FACES IN THE CROWD

Faces in the Crowd

Valeria Luiselli

Translated from the Spanish by
Christina MacSweeney

GRANTA

Granta Publications, 12 Addison Avenue, London W11 4QR

First published in Great Britain by Granta Books 2012

Originally published in Spanish as *Los ingrávidos* by Sexto Piso, Mexico, 2011

A CIP catalogue record for this book is available from the British Library.

1 3 5 7 9 10 8 6 4 2

ISBN 978 1 84708 506 1

Typeset by Avon DataSet Ltd, Bidford on Avon, Warwickshire

Printed and bound in Great Britain by
CPI Group (UK) Ltd, Croydon, CR0 4YY

*Beware! If you play at ghosts,
you become one.*

Anon., *The Kabbalah*

The boy wakes me up:

Do you know where mosquitoes come from, Mama?

Where?

From the shower. During the day they're inside the shower and at night they bite us.

★

It all began in another city and another life. That's why I can't write this story the way I would like to – as if I were still there, still just only that other person. I find it difficult to talk about streets and faces as if I saw them every day. I can't find the correct tenses. I was young, had strong, slim legs.

(I would have liked to start the way Hemingway's *A Moveable Feast* ends.)

★

In that city I lived alone in an almost empty apartment. I slept very little. I ate badly, without much variety. I had a simple life, a routine. I worked as a reader and translator in a small publishing house dedicated to rescuing 'foreign gems'. Nobody bought them, though, because in such an insular culture translation is treated with suspicion. But I liked my work and I believe that for a time I did it well. On Thursdays and Fridays, I did research in libraries, but the first part of the week was reserved for the office. It was a pleasant, comfortable place and, what's more, I was

I

allowed to smoke. Every Monday, I arrived early, full of enthusiasm, carrying a paper cup brimming with coffee. I would say good morning to Minni, the secretary, and then to the chief editor, who was the only editor and therefore the chief. His name was White. I would sit down at my desk, roll a cigarette of Virginia tobacco and work late into the night.

★

In this house live two adults, a baby girl and a little boy. We call him the boy now because, although he's older than his sister, he insists that he's not properly big yet. And he's right. He's older, but he's still small; he's neither the big boy nor the little boy. So he's just the boy.

A few days ago my husband stepped on a dinosaur when he was coming downstairs and there was a cataclysm. Tears, screaming: the dinosaur was shattered beyond repair. Now my T-Rex really has been extincted, sobbed the boy. Sometimes we feel like two paranoid Gullivers, permanently walking on tiptoe so as not to wake anyone up, not to step on anything important and fragile.

★

In winter there were windstorms. But I used to wear miniskirts because I was young. I wrote letters to my acquaintances telling them about my rambles, describing my legs swathed in gray tights, my body wrapped in a red coat with deep pockets. I wrote letters about the cold wind that caressed those legs, compared the freezing air to the bristle of a badly shaved chin, as if the air and a pair of gray legs walking along streets were literary material. When a person has lived alone for a long time, the only way to confirm that they still exist is to express activities and things in an easily shared syntax: this face, these bones that walk, this mouth, this hand that writes.

Now I write at night, when the two children are asleep and it's acceptable to smoke, drink and let draughts in. Before, I used to write all the time, at any hour, because my body belonged to me. My legs were long, strong and slim. It was right to offer them: to whomever, to writing.

★

In that apartment there were only five pieces of furniture: bed, kitchen table, bookcase, desk and chair. In fact, the desk, the chair and the bookcase came later. When I moved in, I found only a bed and a folding aluminum table. There was also a bathtub. But I don't know if that counts as furniture. Little by little, the space began to fill up, though always with temporary objects. The books from the libraries spent the weekends piled high by the bed and disappeared the following Monday, when I took them to the office to write reports on them.

★

A silent novel, so as not to wake the children.

★

Sometimes I bought wine, although the bottle didn't last a single sitting. The bread, lettuce, cheese, whisky and coffee, in that order, lasted a bit longer. And a little longer than all those five together, the oil and soy sauce. But the pens and lighters, for example, came and went like headstrong teenagers determined to demonstrate their complete autonomy. I knew it wasn't a good idea to place the least trust in household objects; as soon as we become accustomed to the silent presence of a thing, it gets broken or disappears. My ties to the people around me were also marked by those two modes of impermanence: breaking up or disappearing.

All that has survived from that period are the echoes of certain conversations, a handful of recurrent ideas, poems I liked and read over and over until I had them off by heart. Everything else is a later elaboration. It's not possible for my memories of that life to have more substance. They are scaffolding, structures, empty houses.

*

In this big house I don't have a place to write. On my worktable, there are nappies, toy cars, Transformers, bibs, rattles, things I still can't figure out. Tiny objects take up all the space. I cross the living room and sit on the sofa with my computer on my lap. The boy comes in:

What are you doing, Mama?
Writing.
Writing just a book, Mama?
Just writing.

*

Novels need a sustained breath. That's what novelists want. No one knows exactly what it means but they all say: a sustained breath. I have a baby and a boy. They don't let me breathe. Everything I write is – has to be – in short bursts. I'm short of breath.

*

I'm going to write a book too, the boy says while we're preparing dinner and waiting for his father to come back from the office.

4

His father hasn't got an office, but he has a lot of appointments and sometimes says: I'm going to the office now. The boy says his father works in the workery. The baby doesn't say anything, but one day she's going to say Pa-pa.

My husband's an architect. He's been designing the same house for almost a year now, over and over, with changes that are, to my mind, imperceptible. The house is going to be built in Philadelphia, quite soon, when my husband finally sends off the definitive plans. In the meantime, they pile up on his desk. Sometimes, I leaf through them, feigning interest. But I don't find it easy to imagine what it's all about, it's difficult to project all those lines into a third dimension. He also leafs through the things I write.

What's your book going to be called? I ask the boy.

It's going to be: *Papa Always Comes Back from the Workery in a Bad Mood.*

*

In our house the electricity cuts out. The fuses have to be changed very frequently. It's a common word in our everyday lexicon now. The electricity cuts out and the boy says: We've got fussy fuses.

I don't think there were any fuses in that apartment, in that other city. I never saw a meter, the electricity never cut out, I never changed a light bulb. They were all fluorescent: they lasted for ever. A Chinese student lived out his life on the opposite window. He used to study until very late at night under his dim light; I also used to stay up late reading. At three in the morning, with oriental precision, he turned out the light in his room. He would switch on the bathroom light and, four minutes later, turn it off again. He never switched on the one in the bedroom. He performed his private rituals in the dark. I liked to wonder about him: did he get completely undressed before getting into bed; did he play with himself; did he do it under the covers or standing by the bed, what was the eye of his cock like; was he thinking about something or watching me, wondering about him, through my kitchen window? When the nocturnal ceremony had finished, I would turn out my light and leave the apartment.

★

We like to think that in this house there's a ghost living with us and watching us. We can't see it, but we believe it appeared a few weeks after we moved in. I was enormous, eight months pregnant. I could scarcely move. I used to drag myself like a sea lion along the wood floor. I set about unpacking the books, organizing them into alphabetical towers. My husband and the boy put them on the freshly painted shelves. The ghost used to knock the towers over. The boy christened it 'Without'.

Why Without?

Just because he's with and without a face, Mama.

The ghost opens and shuts doors. It turns on the stove. The house has a huge stove and lots of doors. My husband tells our son that the ghost bounces a ball against the wall. He is scared to death and immediately curls up in his father's arms, until he swears that it was just a joke. Sometimes Without rocks the baby while I'm writing. Neither of us is frightened by this, and we know it's not a joke. She's the only one who really sees it; she smiles into the empty space with all the charm she's capable of. She's got a new tooth coming through.

★

In this neighborhood the *tamal* seller comes by at eight in the evening. We run to buy half a dozen sweet ones. I don't go outside, but I whistle to him from the front door, putting two fingers in my mouth, and my husband races down the street to catch him. When he comes back, while he's unwrapping the *tamales*, he says: I married a person who whistles. The neighbors also pass by our window and they wave to us. Even though we're newcomers, they're friendly. They all know each other. On Sundays they eat together in the central courtyard. They invite us, but we don't join in the feast; we wave from the living-room window and wish them a good Sunday. It's a group of old houses, all a bit dilapidated or on the point of falling down.

★

I didn't like sleeping alone in my apartment. I lived on the seventh floor. I would lend my apartment to people and to seek out other rooms, borrowed armchairs, shared beds in which to spend the night. I gave copies of my keys to a lot of people. They gave me copies of theirs. Reciprocity, not generosity.

★

On Fridays, though not every Friday, Moby would turn up. He was the first to have the keys. We almost always met in the doorway. I'd be going out to the library and he would arrive to have a bath, because in his house, in a town an hour and a half from the city, there was no hot water. In the beginning, he didn't stay to sleep and I don't know where he did sleep, but he had baths in my tub and in exchange brought me a plant or cooked me something and put it in the fridge. He left notes that I would find in the evening, when I came back to eat dinner: 'I used your shampoo, thanks, M.'

Moby had a weekend job in the city. He forged and sold rare books that he himself produced on a homemade printing press. Well-to-do intellectuals bought them from him at rather unreasonable prices. He also reprinted unique copies of American classics in equally unique formats. (Amazing the obsession gringos have for the unique.) He had an illustrated copy of *Leaves of Grass*, a manuscript of *Walden* he'd written out in pencil, and an audiotape of the essays of Ralph Waldo Emerson read by his Polish grandmother. But the majority of his authors were 'Ohio poets of the twenties and thirties'. That was his niche. He'd developed a theory of hyper-specialization that was working well for him. Of course, it was not he but Adam Smith who had developed it, but he believed the theory was his own. I used to say: That's Adam Smith's pin theory. And Moby would reply: I'm talking about American Poets. The book he was trying to sell around that time was called *Can We Hold Hands Out Here?* He had ten copies and gave me one as a present. It was by a very bad poet. From Cleveland, Ohio, like Moby.

From time to time, before going back home, he came to my apartment to have a second bath and we'd eat the leftovers of whatever he'd cooked on Friday. We talked about the books he'd sold; we talked about books in general. Sometimes, on Sundays, we made love.

★

My husband reads some of this and asks who Moby is. Nobody, I say. Moby is a character.

★

But Moby exists. Or perhaps not. But he existed then. And another person who existed was Dakota, who came to my apartment for the same reason as Moby: she didn't have a shower. She was the second person to have keys. She would turn up for a bath and sometimes stayed to sleep. She also gave me a set of her keys. She lived with her boyfriend in the basement of a big house in

Brooklyn and for months they had been designing a bathroom they never built. I liked spending the night in that basement without a shower, wearing Dakota's nightgowns, trying out her side of the bed.

Dakota worked at night, singing in bars and sometimes in the subway. Her features were like those of a silent-movie star, the eyes two enormous half moons, the mouth very small, haughty eyebrows. She and her boyfriend had a band. He played harmonica. He was from Wyoming – one of those pale gringos who, despite having almost transparent eyes, are handsome. He had a scar that ran from one side of his face to the other. The day I told him I was leaving the city for good because I'd become a ghost, he stroked my forehead. At the time I couldn't tell if that was a reply. I wanted to touch his face, but didn't dare underline the scar.

★

The boy comes back from school and shows me his knee:

Look at my cut.

How did that happen?

I was running around in the playground and a house fell on me.

A hose?

No, a house.

★

This house has a new fridge, a new piece of furniture next to the bed, new plants in terracotta pots. My husband wakes up at midnight from a nightmare. He starts to tell me about it while I dream of something else, but I listen from the beginning, as if I'd never fallen asleep, as if I'd been waiting for the start of that conversa-

9

tion the whole night. He says we're living in a house that grows. New rooms appear, new things, the roof gets higher. The children are there, but always in another room. The boy is in danger and we can't find the baby. At one side of our bed there's a piece of furniture that unfolds and produces music. Inside he finds a tree, a dead tree but deeply rooted into the bottom of a box. In the logic of his dream, it's the tree that produces the sense of doom in the house that grows; he tries to uproot it; the branches reach out and scratch his testicles. My husband cries. I hug him and then get up to go to the children's room. I give the boy a kiss and check the cot to see if the baby is still breathing. She's breathing. But I have no air.

★

I liked cemeteries, parks, the roof terraces of buildings, but most of all cemeteries. In a way, I was living in a perpetual state of communion with the dead. But not in a sordid sense. In contrast, the people around me were sordid. Moby was. Dakota too, sometimes. The dead and I, no. I had read Quevedo and internalized, like a prayer, perhaps too literally, the idea of living in conversation with the dead. I often visited a small graveyard a few blocks from my apartment, because I could read and think there without anyone or anything disturbing me.

★

I go back to writing the novel whenever I'm not busy with the children. I know I need to generate a structure full of holes so that I can always find a place for myself on the page, inhabit it; I have to remember never to put in more than is necessary, never overlay, never furnish or adorn. Open doors, windows. Raise walls and demolish them.

★

When she stayed in my apartment, Dakota did voice exercises with the bucket I used for mopping the floor. She would put her whole head inside and produce really piercing notes, like a badly tuned violin, like a moribund bird, like an old door. Sometimes, when I came back from a few days away, I used to find Dakota lying on the living room floor with the blue bucket beside her. Resting my back, she'd explain.

Why do you always take my bucket out of the bathroom?

So your neighbors can't hear me.

I don't think they can.

So I can hear myself.

Dakota never answered a question directly.

★

My husband draws rapidly; he makes a lot of noise. His pencil scrapes on the paper, he sharpens it every five minutes with the electric pencil sharpener, starts a new piece of paper, walks round his drawing table. He constructs spaces and, as they appear on the sheet, names them: bathroom, spiral staircase, terrace, attic. He stops, sits down. Then he goes to his computer and reproduces the lines using a program that gradually makes the spaces three-dimensional. I can't make spaces from nothing. I can't invent. I only manage to emulate my ghosts, write the way they used to speak, not make noise, narrate our phantasmagoria.

★

Pajarote didn't talk much. He lived in New Brunswick, a horrible town in New Jersey, and drove to Manhattan in his old car every

II

Wednesday because he was taking a course at NYU on Thursday mornings. His real name was Abelardo, but everyone called him Pajarote – literally, big bird – after the Sesame Street character, whom he resembled in physical but certainly not mental stature. He was a philosophy student, and took life philosophically. The only complaint I ever heard him make was about the way non-Spanish speakers were always trying to put either a hard *j* or a wimpish *h* in the middle of his name. He spent every Wednesday night at my place. I liked sleeping there when he was around. He used to wrap a long, hairless arm around me. But we never made love. It was an unspoken pact that protected our friendship. Every Thursday, he'd get up early and buy bread and Coke in the supermarket on the corner. We would eat breakfast together without saying a word. One day I broke the silence and asked him what his course was about.

It's to do with vagueness, he said, chewing a piece of bread.

Just that? Vagueness?

Well, vagueness and fuzzy temporal boundaries.

I thought it was a joke, I teased him a bit, but he said: It's cutting-edge analytical philosophy. His classes that month would cover puzzles about temporary coincidence, where the example was a cat, now with a tail, now without a tail. Pajarote continued chewing as he was going on about cats and vagueness, so that small archipelagos of spittle and crumbs accumulated in the corners of his mouth.

Is it the same cat? he asked, after a long explanation which I'd stopped listening to. I nodded, and then said no, or that in fact I didn't know. Perhaps it's like Hemingway said: One cat just leads to another. Pajarote didn't laugh. He never laughed. Or perhaps he did, but never at my jokes. He was more intelligent than me, more serious than me. He was very tall and had long, hairless arms.

★

That apartment gradually filled up with plants, silent presences which from time to time reminded me that the world required care and perhaps even affection. There were practically never any flowers. There were leaves, yes: some green and many yellow. I'd see a handful of withered leaves on the floor and feel guilty; I picked them up, put water in all the pots, but then forgot about them for another couple of weeks.

There's nothing so ill-advised as attributing a metonymic value to inanimate things. If you think the condition of a plant in a pot is a reflection of the condition of your soul, or worse, that of a loved one, you'll be condemned to disillusion or perpetual paranoia.

★

That's what White used to say. He didn't have keys to my apartment. But he went there twice. On both occasions, after a couple of drinks, he told me the same story. There was a tree outside his house in which he was constantly seeing his dead wife. He didn't actually see her, but he knew she was there. Like fear in a nightmare, like a sudden sadness that fills long afternoons. Every night, when he got home, he said goodnight to her, to the tree, to her in the tree. He didn't speak. He just thought about her as he passed the tree and grazed it with his fingertips. It was a way of saying goodbye, again, each time.

One night he forgot. He went into his apartment, brushed his teeth and got into bed. Then he realized that he'd forgotten his wife. He was stricken with guilt and went outside again. He didn't put on his shoes. He hugged the tree and cried until his socks, feet and knees were soaked by the snow covering the street. When he went back inside, he didn't take his socks off to sleep.

★

The boy asks:
    What's your book about, Mama?
    It's a ghost story.
    Is it frightening?
    No, but it's a bit sad.
    Why? Because the ghosts are dead?
    No, they're not dead.
    Then they're not very ghosty.
    No, they're not ghosts.

★

There are different versions of the story. The version I liked was the one White told me when we'd been working late in the office and had to wait over an hour for a train. Standing on the platform, listening for the shuddering in the interior of things produced by the imminent arrival of a moving train, he told me that one day, in that very station, the poet Ezra Pound had seen his friend Henri Gaudier-Brzeska, who had been killed in a trench in Neuville-Saint-Vaast a few months before. Pound was waiting on the platform, leaning against a pillar, when the train finally pulled in. The doors of the carriage opened and he saw the face of his friend appear among the people. In a few seconds, the carriage filled with other faces, and Brzeska's was buried in the crowd. Shocked, Pound didn't move for several moments, until first his knees and then his entire body gave way. Leaning his whole weight against the pillar, he slid down until he felt the concrete caress of the ground on his ass. He took out a notebook and began to write. That same night, in a diner in the south of the city, he completed a poem of over three hundred lines. The next day he reread it and thought it too long. He went back every day to the same station, the same pillar, to lop, cut, mutilate the poem. It had to be exactly as brief as his dead friend's appearance, exactly as startling.

After a month of work, removing everything extraneous, only two poignant lines survived, comparing faces in the crowd to petals on a dark bough

★

Dakota and I met in the toilet of a bar called Café Moto. She was making up her face with a sponge when I went to the sink to wash my hands. I never wash my hands in public toilets, but the woman touching up the future face of Dakota with a sponge seemed to me unsettling and I wanted a closer look. So I washed my hands.

★

The publishing house was at 555 Edgecombe Avenue but I spent half the week in libraries around the city, looking for books by Latin American writers worth translating or re-issuing. White was sure that, following Bolaño's success in the American market some five years before, there would be another Latin American boom. A paid passenger on the runaway train of his enthusiasm, I brought him a backpack full of books every Monday, and spent my working hours writing detailed reports on every one of them. Inés Arredondo, Josefina Vicens, Carlos Díaz Dufoo Jr, Sergio Pitol, nothing caught his interest.

Weren't you a friend of Bolaño? White shouted from his desk (I worked at a small desk beside his, so the shouting was unnecessary but it made him feel like a real editor). He took a long drag on his cigarette and continued in the same mode: Haven't you got any letters from him or an interview or something we could publish? he shouted. No, White, I never met him. Shame. Did you hear that, Minni? We have the honor of working with the only Latin American woman who wasn't a friend of Bolaño.

Who's he, chief? asked Minni, who never knew anything about anything. He's the most popular dead Chilean writer ever. His name gets dropped more often than coins into a wishing well.

★

I walked very little in that city where everyone goes for walks. I went from my apartment to the office, from the office to some library. And, of course, to the cemetery a few blocks from my house. One day, in her eternal eagerness to bring about a change in me, my sister Laura sent me an e-mail from Philadelphia. It said simply: 115 West 95th Street. Laura lived in Philadelphia with her wife Enea. They still live there. They're active people, pleased with themselves. Enea is Argentinian and teaches at Princeton. Laura and Enea belong to all sorts of groups and organizations; they're academics; they're left-wing, they're vegetarians. This year they're going to climb Kilimanjaro.

I left my apartment, bundled up in my gray tights and the red coat with enormous pockets. I coiled a scarf around my neck and walked directly to the address Laura had sent me.

The location existed, but it was the number of an imaginary house. Instead of doors, windows and steps, there was a brick wall on which someone had painted a window frame, a vase of flowers, a cat snoozing on the sill, a woman looking out into the street. Too late, I realized it was one of Laura's sophisticated jokes. A *trompe l'œil* that functioned as a trope for my lifestyle in that city. I don't know what Laura would say now that my only walks are from the kitchen to the living room, from the upstairs bathroom to the children's bedroom. But Laura knows nothing of this, nor will she be told.

On the way back to my apartment, I stopped at a rummage sale outside a church. I bought a 1950s' anthology of modern American and British poetry for one dollar and a small bookcase with four shelves for ten. I used to like walking along the streets carrying furniture. It's something I don't do anymore. But when I did, I felt like a person with a purpose. Back in my apartment, I put the bookcase in the center of the only wall in the living room without windows and placed my new book on the top shelf. From time to time I'd open the book, choose one of the poems and copy it out. When I left the house to go to the office, I took the sheet of paper with me to memorize the poem. William Carlos Williams, Joshua Zvorsky, Emily Dickinson and Charles Olson. I had a theory; I'm not sure if it was my own but it worked for me. Public spaces, such as streets and subway stations, became inhabitable as I assigned them some value and imprinted an experience on them. If I recited a snatch of *Paterson* every time I walked along a certain avenue, eventually that avenue would sound like William Carlos Williams. The entrance to the subway at 116th Street was Emily Dickinson's:

> Presentiment is that long shadow on the lawn
> Indicative that suns go down;
> The notice to the startled grass
> That darkness is about to pass.

★

Milk, nappy, vomiting and regurgitation, cough, snot and abundant dribble. The cycles now are short, repetitive and imperative. It's impossible to try to write. The baby looks at me from her high chair: sometimes with resentment, sometimes with admiration. Maybe with love, if we are indeed able to love at that age. She produces sounds that will have a hard time adapting themselves to Spanish, when she learns to speak it. Closed vowels, guttural opinions. She speaks a bit like the characters in a Lars von Trier movie.

*

I write: I met Moby on the subway. And though that is the truth, it's not really credible, because normal people, like Moby and I, never meet on the subway. Instead, I could write: I met Moby on a park bench. A park bench is any park, any bench. And that, perhaps, is a good thing. Perhaps it's right that words contain nothing, or almost nothing. That their content is, at the very least, variable. Typically, the bench would be green and made of wood. So, not to be predictable, I should write: Moby was reading a newspaper on one of the white, slightly battered concrete benches in Morningside Park. A bent, submissive gardener was trimming the hedge with a pair of clippers. It was 10 a.m. and the park was almost empty, like the word 'park' and the word 'bench'. Maybe I ought to explain why I was crossing the park from east to west at ten in the morning. I'd lie: I was going to mass. I was going to the cemetery, or the supermarket, which perhaps are more or less the same thing. Or better: I'd spent the night sleeping on one of those benches.

But what's the use of all that if the truth is: I met Moby on the subway. I was reading some book whose title I can't now re-member – *A orillas del Hudson* by Martín Luis Guzmán, perhaps – and he was next to me, turning the pages of a fascinating book with stills from films by Jonas Mekas. I asked him where he'd found the book and he told me he'd produced it himself. He handed me a card for a printer's, his printer's, in a town outside the city.

*

It was very easy to disappear. Very easy to put on a red coat, switch off all the lights, go somewhere else, not go back to sleep anywhere. No one was waiting for me in any bed. They are now.

Now I know that when I go into the children's room, the baby will catch my smell and shiver in her cot, because some secret place in her body is teaching her to demand her part of what belongs to us both, the threads that sustain and separate us.

Then, when I go into my own room, my husband will also demand his portion of me and I will give myself up to the indefinite, sudden, serene pleasure of his touch.

★

Moby had a big nineteenth-century house in a town that was soulless, but pleasant in its puritan way, not far from the city. The house didn't have electricity or running water. Moby lived there, lived alone. He heated up cans of soup on a kerosene stove and slept on a mattress on the floor. His bedside book was the biography of Santayana. He got up at five every day, made a cup of green tea and worked at the printing press until after midday. He lived that way of his own volition, not because there were no other options. There are two types of people: those who just live and those who design their lives. Moby was in the latter category. You had to take off your shoes before entering his house and put on Japanese slippers. There was something affected in that life, in the over-aesthetization of that reality, designed as if to be viewed through a lens. I definitely did not fit into Moby's filmic life. That's why I accepted the green tea, why I let Moby undress me, wrap me in a Japanese robe and then undress me again in order to run his bony hands, his narrow nose, his thin, almost invisible lips over my body. That's why I slept naked on that mattress next to the printing press, and hurried away the following morning. I was in the habit of carrying around two sets of keys to my apartment – one in my bag and the other in the pocket of my red coat in case I lost one – and, before going, I left a set for Moby, on top of a note with my address.

★

The baby's asleep. The boy, my husband and I sit on the stairs, facing the front door. He asks his father:

Papa, what's a wasp?

It's a dangerous bee.

And a sperm whale?

It's a Moby Dick.

★

One night I acquired a writing desk for my empty apartment. I didn't buy it. But I didn't steal it either. I suppose I should say that it was found for me. I was in a smoker's bar. I'd spent the evening rolling cigarettes, browsing through a terribly boring anthology of Mexican poets – friends of Octavio Paz and, perhaps for that reason alone, translated into English – while waiting for Dakota to finish her last set in a nearby bar. When my mind momentarily wandered from my reading, I had the sensation that someone was watching me from outside. Through the window, I saw Dakota on the sidewalk, sitting on something, straightening her stockings. She waved and beckoned me over. I paid. Dakota was sitting on an antique writing desk, her dainty red high-heeled shoes beside her.

I found you a writing desk, she said, so you can write your stuff.

And how am I going to get it home?

We'll carry it. See, I've taken my heels off.

First we dragged it, then we tried carrying it by the corners, one at either end. The task seemed impossible: the apartment was over thirty blocks away. Finally, we got underneath and rested it on our heads and the palms of our hands. Dakota sang the rest of the way home. I did the backing vocals. We got blisters.

★

I can only write during the day if the baby is having a nap beside me. She's learned to grab anything that comes near her and clings to my right hand to sleep. I write for a while with the left one. The capitals are really difficult. Two or three times, I make an attempt to get my hand back, gently sliding it from between the bars of her fingers, and moving it to the keyboard to type another line. She wakes up and cries, looks at me resentfully. I give her back my hand and she loves me again.

★

So I could work at the new writing desk, I took one of the office chairs to my apartment. Nobody used it, no one was likely to notice, it had been left forgotten in the bathroom for months and its only function was to hold a roll of toilet paper. It was made of pale wood; slender and fragile. I painted it blue in case White came back some day and recognized it. I put it in front of the new writing desk and wrote a letter to my sister Laura. It began: 'I live opposite a park where the children are children and play baseball.'

★

The boy plays hide-and-seek in this house full of nooks and crannies. It's a different version of the game. He hides and my husband and I have to seek. We have to bring the baby with us and when we finally find him under the bed or in a closet, he shouts, 'Found!' and the baby has to start laughing. If the baby doesn't laugh, we have to begin all over again.

★

One Friday afternoon, while I was in the Columbia University library looking through books to take to the office on Monday, I came across a letter from the Mexican poet Gilberto Owen to his friend and fellow-writer Xavier Villaurrutia: 'I live at 63 Morningside Ave. There's a plant pot in the right hand window that looks like a lamp. It's got oval-shaped green flames...' The letter came from his collected works, *Obras*, and in it Owen listed the objects in a room he was renting in Harlem: writing desk, pictures, plant, magazines, a piano. The address he gave Villaurrutia caught my eye. The building had to be only a few blocks from the library, and very close to my apartment. I didn't even finish reading the letter. I left the other books I'd selected in a pile, checked out *Obras* and left.

After three in the afternoon that neighborhood used to smell of salt: the tears and sweat of the black and Latino children coming out of school, scabs on their knees, spittle and snot on the sleeves of their sweaters. One girl, broad as she was long, was working on a drawing propped up against the trunk of a tree in Morningside Park. In one hand she had a chicken leg, which she bit, or rather sucked, from time to time, and between the thumb and index finger of her other hand she held the green wax crayon with which she was completing the drawing. A boy came up behind her and whacked the back of her legs with his schoolbag – the two plump knees buckled– then grabbed her crayon. She recovered herself, lunged at him and screamed, You madafaka, then beat his face with the chicken leg until he fell to the ground.

I walked to Owen's building. I'd often seen it on my way to the subway without knowing he'd lived there. It was a red stone building, similar to all the others in the block, with large windows overlooking the park. When I stopped in front of it, an elderly man was entering the building so I slipped in after him. I went up to the first floor, the second, and continued upwards. The man stopped on the third floor, turned to smile at me – Afternoon, ma'am; Afternoon, sir – and went into an apartment. I carried on up to the fourth and fifth floor, until my breath and the stairs ran out, went through a door leading to the roof terrace and closed it behind me. I lit a cigarette in a sunny corner and waited for something to happen.

As the world didn't register any changes, I started reading the book I'd just taken out of the library, waiting for some propitious signal. Nothing happened; I went on reading and smoking until it began to get dark. After a few hours, I'd finished all the letters in the volume, the entire collection of poetry in *Perseo vencido*, and the last of my tobacco, so I decided to go home. I stood up, looking for somewhere to get rid of my handful of cigarette ends. In a corner of the terrace there was a plant in a pot and I went across to bury them in it. I sat down on a stack of newspapers someone had tied up with string, as if for recycling, and dug a hole. Then I realized that the plant pot, like the one Owen described to Villaurrutia, resembled a lamp. The plant in the pot – perhaps a small tree – was withered. It couldn't possibly be the same one Owen referred to in his letter, but it was, I thought, some kind of signal, the signal I'd been waiting for. I was overtaken by that same excitement babies display when they confirm their existence in a mirror.

It wasn't my habit to take things that didn't belong to me. Just sometimes, some things. Sometimes, quite a lot of things. But when I saw that small, dead tree on Owen's roof, it seemed to me that I had to take it home, care for it, at least for the rest of the winter. Later, perhaps when spring came round again, I could return it to the roof. It was getting darker. I made my way to the door, carrying the pot, ready to go home. But the door had no handle on the outside and I could find no way to open it.

I once read in a book by Saul Bellow that the difference between being alive and being dead is just a matter of viewpoint: the living look from the center outwards, the dead from the periphery to some sort of center. Perhaps I froze, perhaps I died of hypothermia. In any case, it was the first night I had to spend with Gilberto Owen's ghost. If I believed in turning points, which I don't, I'd say that I began that night to live as if inhabited by another possible life that wasn't mine, but one which, simply by the use of imagination, I could give myself up to completely. I started looking inwards from the outside, from someplace to nowhere. And I still do, even now, when my husband is sleeping, and the baby and the boy are asleep, and I could also be asleep, but am not, because sometimes I feel that my bed is not a bed, these hands are not my hands. I buttoned my coat up to the neck, arranged the sun-soaked papers on the concrete, forming a mat of news that protected me a little. Before sinking my hands into my deep pockets, I put the book into my backpack and used it as a pillow. I placed the plant pot at my feet and lay face up on the ground.

At daybreak, I went to the edge of the roof and sat there, hoping that someone would soon come out of the building. My hands were blue, my lips chapped. Around nine in the morning – the sun was beginning to warm my back – a girl came out with a bicycle. I shouted down to her. The girl turned her head and waved. It was the same fat child with the green wax crayon I'd seen the day before. I begged, promised candy, crayons and chicken legs in reward for her help. She left her bicycle propped up against the front steps and went back into the building. She took ages to come up, prolonging my agony. I imagined she would go to fetch her mother, her father, her grandparents, all the residents of the building would come up to lynch me and I would have to explain that – What would I say? – that I'd got lost, was sweeping the roof, that I was Mexican, a translator – Sorry, sir; Sorry, ma'am – or that perhaps there was nothing strange about my being up there on their roof on a Saturday morning.

The roof-top door, a thin metal sheet, began to shake slightly and then burst open. The girl had come up alone. She stood there, gazing blankly at me, and asked:

Are you the ghost that lives up here?

No, I just came up to water my plant early this morning and got locked out.

But are you a ghost?

No, ghosts don't exist. I'm Mexican.

We're from the Dominican Republic. My mom doesn't let us come up here because of the ghost.

She's right.

What are you going to do with that dead tree?

I'm going to take it to the tree doctor.

She turned and I followed her, carrying the pot. We went slowly downstairs. Outside, a bunch of fat kids were waiting for her. I put the pot down for a moment and we shook hands, rather awkwardly on my part.

What's your name? I asked.

Dolores Preciado, but they call me Do.

I picked up the pot again. The other children watched me pass, carrying the dead tree. They laughed, shamelessly made fun of me: the natural cruelty of children becomes more intense when they are fat. I crossed to the other side of the park and Do shouted to me:

Tree doctors, they don't exist either!

When I got to my apartment, I put the plant pot next to the writing desk. Before taking a bath, before making coffee, before having a pee, I sat down to write a feverish report on Gilberto Owen's *Sindbad el varado*. The Chinese student was drinking soup at his worktable.

★

25

Some evenings, my husband and I work together in the living room, spurred on by the whisky, the tobacco and the promise of late-night sex. He says that we only work at night so we can smoke and drink in peace. We'll get to the bed, after making a few additions to our respective documents, as excited as two strangers who have met for the first time and don't tell each other anything or demand explanations. The *tabula rasa* of the pages and plans, the anonymity the multiple voices of the writing offer me, the freedom his empty spaces give to him.

★

In that apartment, there was nothing. There weren't even ghosts. There were heaps of half-alive plants and a dead tree.

★

In this house we often run out of water. The boy says that it's the ghost who uses up the reserves in the cistern. He says it's a ghost who died of thirst and that's why it drinks all the water in the house.

★

Pajarote invited me to dinner to celebrate his birthday. We went to a French place. I knew that, for the gringos, French means elegant, so I was well-dressed and on my best behavior. I didn't order much food, onion soup and clams; he had duck. I babbled on about the plant I'd taken from the roof of Owen's old building, about the girl called Do who'd saved me, about Owen's possible lives in 1920s' Harlem, about the new writing desk and its chair, about Moby and the Japanese robes and how sad I'd felt making love on a mattress, next to a printing press, with a man

26

with a big nose. Pajarote looked at me in silence.

You've got a bit of burnt onion on your teeth, he said when I finally paused.

We finished eating and were brought liqueurs in tiny glasses. When we'd polished off the drinks, I put the glasses in my bag. They were very pretty glasses. Pajarote looked at me quizzically. It's my birthday, he said, please don't steal today. I'll buy you the glasses. And he called the waiter over and bought them for me.

★

The baby laughs out loud for the first time. She makes a noise like a whale and her voice immediately breaks into four abrupt, light, resonant gusts of laughter.

★

White wasn't impressed by my first report on Owen. He left a note stuck on the screen of my computer: 'Bring me something that really can be translated into English and return the wooden chair you stole from the bathroom, then we'll talk about what we might be able to do with your Owen. Yours, W.'

Unlike the majority of gringo publishers, White was not monolingual. And in contrast to the majority of gringos who speak Spanish and have spent some time in Latin America and think that gives them a kind of international third-world experience which confers on them the intellectual and moral qualifications for – I don't quite know what – White really did understand the fucked-up mechanisms of Latin American literary history. Faced with his reluctance, the most natural thing for me to do would have been to take note and leave Owen alone.

The boy to his father:
  Do octopuses have little mobydicks?
  I'm working.
  And shrimps? And sea sponges?
  The boy's father thinks for a moment and then:
  Shrimps *are* little-dicks.

★

When the doctor told me my second pregnancy was 'high risk', I stopped just about everything: smoking, drinking, walking, writing, breathing. I was afraid the baby wouldn't be fully developed: the spine incomplete, crooked; the nervous system disconnected; I was afraid of mental retardation, delayed learning, blindness, sudden infant death syndrome. I'm not religious, but one day when I was in the street I had a panic attack – my sister Laura explained later that that was what it was – and I had to stop in a church. I went in to pray. That is, I went in to ask for something. I prayed for the unformed baby, for the love of its father and brother, for my fear. Something in the silence convinced me that there was a heart in my belly, a heart with an aorta, full of blood; a sponge, a beating organ.

★

A dense, porous novel. Like a baby's heart.

★

In the copy of Owen's *Obras* I borrowed from the library there was a section with photographs, placed more or less at random among the pages of *Novela como nube*. One of the photos caught my eye. Two-thirds of Owen's profile occupied almost the whole space. The wide forehead and a strand of wavy hair. A thin nose, practically a beak. The eyebrow shading an almost non-existent eyelid, the soft, sleepy eye. Scarcely a trace of upper lip. All the rest, black. An almost faceless man. I carefully tore out the photo and placed it on one of the branches of the dead tree, next to my writing desk – anyway, I had no intention of returning the book to the library.

★

My husband and I watch a film with the children. It's called *Raining Hamburgers*. It's a ridiculous story. The baby, who is the most sensible of the four, falls asleep after a few minutes; the boy stays awake only a little longer. We carry them to their cot and bed respectively, and watch them sleep. In some way, we love each other in them, through them. Perhaps more through them than through ourselves – as if since their arrival the empty space that brought us together and separated us had been filled with something, something that was neither him nor me, that now seemed essential to our self-justification. We kiss their foreheads, close the door of their room. We lie on our bed and finish watching the film, unable to sleep.

★

I sometimes slept in an armchair on the tenth floor of my building because there was too little air and too much noise in my apartment. There was always someone or something else there: Moby taking a bath, Pajarote breakfasting on toast, Dakota with the bucket; there was the echo of White's sad story, the menace of the live plants, a dead tree and a photo of the ghost of Gilberto Owen – all those things stopped me sleeping.

★

One afternoon, I took White to Saint Nick's, a bar not far from the office, to try to convince him of Owen's potential. We'd been talking about St John of the Cross the whole day, discussing the *Spiritual Canticle*, because White was going to bring out a bilingual edition with an English translation by the well-known American poet Joshua Zvorsky. The original manuscript was incomplete, so we had to restore the missing sections. We stayed there well into the evening, working on some of the Bride's stanzas, and ordering more whisky.

> My Beloved is the mountains,
> The solitary wooded valleys,
> The strange isles,
> The sonorous rivers,
> The whistling of amorous gales;

Do you prefer 'sonorous rivers' or 'roaring torrents'? he asked.
  Neither.
  How about the valleys: 'wooded valleys' or 'bosky valleys'?
  Bosky rhymes with Zvorsky and whisky. Well, maybe not whisky. And what are 'amorous gales'? I think that's meaningless, White.
  Breezes. Gales should be breezes.

> The tranquil night
> At the approaches of the dawn,
> The silent music,
> The murmuring solitude,
> The supper which revives, and enkindles love.

'Enkindles love' is really shitty, White.

30

'Rekindles.' It's 'rekindles'. Yeah, that's good.

Every so often, we left our drinks on the bar and went outside to smoke. White's enthusiasm was contagious. Perhaps mine could be too. So, during one of those pauses, I tried telling him a lie:

Did you know Gilberto Owen used to come to this very bar?

No, I don't think so. This place opened in the thirties or forties and according to your report Owen was in New York earlier than that.

All right, he didn't come here, but did you know he was a friend of Federico García Lorca?

St John, let's stick to St John. How would you translate that beautiful bit of alliteration: '*Un no sé qué que quedan balbuciendo*'?

Not sure: 'A nonsensical I know not what'? 'A something I know not what'?

Someone must have spiked my drink while we were outside smoking. When we returned to the bar, I knocked back my whisky and suddenly could hardly understand a word White was saying. I looked on in silence as he talked about William Carlos Williams, Zvorsky and Pound. He quoted lines from memory and laughed uncontrollably. I laughed with him, unsure what it was all about. A blue halo began to pulsate around his head. I reached out my hand, trying to touch it.

What's wrong with you? he asked.

The halo! You're St John, White.

I'm going to take a leak, then we're off, he said.

The waiter behind the bar seemed very tall, stretched out. He had long teeth, a devilish smile. People were laughing. White was taking ages. I closed my eyes for a moment. When I opened them, I saw William Carlos Williams beside me, wearing enormous glasses, inspecting the vagina of a miniature woman lying on a napkin on the bar; there was the poet Zvorsky sitting at a table, conducting an imaginary orchestra; Ezra Pound hanging in a cage at the corner of the counter and García Lorca tossing him peanuts, which he accepted gleefully. Let's go, I heard White say behind me. I insisted it was my call, but my wallet had been stolen. He paid and we started for the door. Before going out, I saw Owen, looking terribly sad, eating peanut debris underneath Ezra Pound's cage.

It was a long way to the hospital, the solitary bosky valleys. I looked at my thighs clad in the gray tights, trying not to lose my sense of reality. We walked along the frosty, bosky, Zvorsky sidewalk. All the while, White rattled on about the tree outside his house. He wanted to cut it down. My legs were the color of sidewalks in winter: they were like an extension of the sidewalk. I told White about the tree in the plant pot I'd stolen from Owen's roof. I looked at my legs to avoid seeing anything else. I was a gray woman, a sidewalk-woman. St John, St Owen, let's stick to St John. The tights, the sidewalk: my Beloved is the mountains. I didn't know any prayers, but reciting St John's lines in my head kept me close to something, some tangible center, while White's careworn face transmuted into umpteen possible faces, each with its unsettling blue halo.

Will they put me in jail if someone sees me cutting down the tree? White was asking.

I think so, White.

The sonorous rivers: sidewalks, steps and frost. The whistling of amorous breezes; the rhythm of my footsteps in the snow. In the logic of the sick person, of the idiot, the mad, everything is about to fall into place.

Would you help me cut it down?

What?

The tree.

But nothing ever falls into place. At the hospital, they thought I'd taken the drugs of my own free will. To calm me down, they gave me Valium: the tranquil night. Perhaps I died again, like I died that day on Owen's roof. I slept: at the approaches of the dawn. I don't know if it was hours or minutes: the silent music, the murmuring solitude. When I woke up I asked White for his cell phone and rang my sister to tell her what had happened. She explained: You had a panic attack. I said: No, I was drugged and robbed, and a *no sé qué que quedan balbuciendo*.

White stayed at my bedside until I stabilized. Around midday, we left the hospital and he walked me to the door of my building. Still a little dopey from the Valium and very grateful to White, I promised to help him fell the tree. He promised to read the notes I'd made about Owen more carefully. Just do me a bit more research so we can write a biographical sketch, he said, giving me a hug. He also told me I could keep the chair, which, anyhow, no one used. I entered the building, greeted the doorman, went up to my apartment and brushed my teeth. Or perhaps I didn't brush my teeth.

★

We've all come down with a virus. The first to get it was the boy. Then the baby. Now my husband and I, but worse. The boy says we've got a virus each, so altogether, that's four viri.

★

In that country people complained and filed reports. They called the police. Dakota came to see me a few days after the incident in the bar. She asked:

Have you reported it?

No. What for?

She made the call, dramatizing the events, putting on a foreign accent. Last night some men drugged and robbed me, she said. They used my credit card and cleaned out my account. Dakota was very good when she was dramatizing. A few hours later, two uniformed cops turned up at my apartment. They took coffee in the dining room and notes in a notebook. The detective will call you in a few days, they said before going. I liked the idea of a detective calling me one day. The younger of the two handed me a piece of paper with his full name, phone number and a heart with a smiley face in the center. I propped it up on the branches of the tree, next to my writing desk. Dakota and I got a little tipsy and watched a Jim Jarmusch movie.

★

My husband likes Stanley Kubrick and zombie movies, all zombie movies. The four of us have been in bed with a bug, alternating Kubrick and zombie movies. I can't understand how he can like the two things at the same time. I confront him: It's as if you like men and women at the same time. The boy contributes: It's as if you liked Corn Pops with milk.

★

The detective rang my house a few days later. It was Sunday. Detective Matias speaking, he said. The following day, I went to see him in his office in a federal building opposite St Mary's Primary School. In the reception, some wooden chairs and a cork board with that week's notices: photos of missing people, emergency numbers, lists of possible offences, a typed announcement about a Catholic priest who'd been beaten about the head with a baseball bat wielded by the members of a gang. Again and again: facial and cranial injuries.

The waiting room smelled of piss. A secretary directed me to a room in which, presumably, interrogations were carried out. A squat little man with an Andean face and a Bronx accent came in.

He was the caricature of a detective: hat, raincoat and a toothpick. Detective Matias said:

Cup of coffee?

★

I don't like zombie films. Why did you write that I like zombie films?

Because.

Please, cut the zombies.

★

One night, when we had to finish reading some manuscripts, White invited me to have pizza at his place. We worked late and, around four in the morning, White fell asleep with his head resting on the table. I catnapped in an armchair until dawn, reading a book called *That*, by Joshua Zvorsky, which I had found on the top of one of the many towers of books White had piled around the house. I listened to the sound of his placid snoring across the table. White had an affinity for Zvorsky. And there I was, sitting at the break of day, reading his poetry. I didn't understand much, but it occurred to me that this could be my means of convincing White about the importance of Gilberto Owen. That's the way literary recognition works, at least to a certain degree. It's all a matter of rumor, a rumor that multiplies like a virus until it becomes a collective affinity.

★

Over the next few months, I returned to the Columbia University library several times in search of books, newspapers or archives, whatever might cast a little light on the period Owen spent in New York. Nothing. But I took out Zvorsky's *That* and read it with great care.

On White's recommendation, I began to keep a record of anything that bore any relationship to Owen. I made notes on yellow Post-its and when I got back to my apartment, propped them on the branches of the dead tree, so as not to forget, so as to return some day and organize them. The idea was that when the tree was bursting with notes, they'd begin to fall from their own weight. I would gather them up as they fell and write the story of Owen's life in that same order. The first one was:

Note: The NY Subway was constructed in 1904, the year of Owen's birth.

I still have these notes. When we moved to this house, I took them out of the envelope I'd put them in years before, when I left that city, and stuck them on the wall opposite my writing desk. The boy is learning to read and spends hours by the wall trying to find some meaning in those Post-its. He doesn't ask me questions. My husband, on the other hand, wants to know everything.

★

Dakota used to sing in three or four different bars and, when she needed extra cash, she sang in the subway. One night I went to see her in a station on the 1 line. I took my wooden chair and placed it against the platform wall, facing the rails. Dakota and her boyfriend had installed themselves in the middle of the passage. He was playing the guitar beside her and looking at her the way ventriloquists do their dummies, the way parents look at their children. The trains went by to one side of them. It was obvious that he despised and respected her at the same time. The trains

36

stopped in front of me. He adored her and was afraid of her. He played well that night, and she sang as I had never heard her before. But none of the hundreds of people who alighted from the trains stopped to listen. Dakota's public persona was a mixture of Vincent Gallo's languid elegance and Kimya Dawson's rakish ease. She had a sturdy build and moved with the grace of a cabbage, but the timbre of her voice carried along the platform and pierced my head with the blunt violence of sorrows that run deep. A train stopped. Behind Dakota I thought I saw Owen's face among the many other faces of the subway. It was only for a second. But I was sure he had seen me too.

★

Note (Owen to Celestino Gorostiza): 'New York has to be seen from the viewpoint of the subway. The flat horizontal perspective vanishes in there. A bulky landscape begins, with the double depth, or what they call the fourth dimension, of time.'

★

Dakota liked my dead tree. And I liked her liking it.

It keeps me company and we talk about lots of things, she once said.

And what does it say to you?

It doesn't say anything, it's dead.

She watered it while I was away on a work trip. Spring had arrived and flowers were blooming everywhere. The narcissi are always first, Dakota explained, that way they do some kind of poetic justice to their namesake's eagerness to be seen. But the tree wasn't budding. When I got back from my trip, Dakota had made me fish and spring greens. We drank a bottle of wine. She told me she wanted to leave her boyfriend, and asked if she could

37

live with me for a while, until she found a place of her own.

Why are you leaving him?

I'm not sure.

Dakota had beautiful features. She liked to say she had a ravaged face – she'd read Marguerite Duras in her early twenties and had got the idea that beauty was a French kind of thing. And perhaps that was true. Dakota looked a little like Anaïs Nin and had her hair cut short like Jean Seberg in *À bout de souffle*.

★

Moby wasn't interested in the tree holding Owen's future story. He used to hang his gloves on it when he came to the apartment, as if it were a hat stand.

★

I never unearthed anything important or revealing during my library searches, but I lied to White. I told him that, in the small, disorganized library of Columbia University's Casa Hispánica, I had found an original, badly typed and barely legible, in which were a series of annotated translations of poems by Owen. The translations were almost certainly by Zvorsky, I said: They're signed JZ&GO. It was the most unlikely of all possible lies about Owen, and White never believed it, but he decided to go along with me. I promised to bring him my own literal transcriptions of the text. I was hanging my hopes on the idea that, by making Owen sound like Zvorsky, I could convince White to publish him.

★

Dakota moved in with me. She turned up with a grass-green suitcase in one hand and a new bucket in the other. When I didn't spend the night elsewhere, we both slept in my bed, though Dakota almost always got back very late from work. She would get into bed naked and put an arm around my equally bare waist. She had soft, heavy breasts; small nipples. She used to say she had philosophical nipples.

★

My husband has started reading some of these pages again. Did you use to sleep with women? he asks.

★

If you really want to get under a person's skin, make an accusation about their moral hygiene. That's what Salvatore used to say. He was an elderly biologist from Naples who lived on the tenth floor of my building. Salvatore and I met in the elevator. He had a tangle of white hair on his head, a hooked nose, enormous nostrils edged with crusts of snot. We were both going to the basement, where the washing machines and the trashcans were located. I was carrying a bag of dirty laundry; he his trash. He wasn't carrying trash, he had junk in a gray suitcase. Stuff, he said when I asked him what he had in there. Standing by the trashcans, he took out his things, separated them into small piles, and slowly deposited them in the different containers. Standing by one of the machines, taking longer than usual to carry out my modest hygiene ritual, I watched him out of the corner of my eye. The last thing he took out was an old record player. I went over and asked if it worked. Yes, it did. He let me take it back with me. I'll give you some records later, he said. He never kept his promise. But one day he invited me to dinner on the tenth floor.

★

But have you ever slept with a woman? my husband asks again. No, never, I reply. I wouldn't know how.

★

Note: Owen used to weigh himself every day before getting on the subway. There was a weighing machine in the 116th Street station that confirmed his belief that he was disintegrating: 126 pounds, 125 pounds. He never knew how many kilos he lost a week.

★

Before we moved to this house, my husband, the boy and I lived in a tiny, dark, ground-floor flat. The only place with any natural light was the bathroom, where we had an old washing machine next to the bathtub, and a small cupboard full of medicines, jars of cream we never used and sometimes coffee cups and dirty socks that had lost their pair. The day we did the pregnancy test my husband sat on the washing machine while I peed. The bathroom was our adult corner and those were our places, the toilet-seat and the washing machine: there we made decisions, there we quarreled so the boy wouldn't hear. I bungled the first test and he had to go and buy another. While he was out, I put all the clothes I could find scattered around the apartment on to wash. I added the tea towels, our sheets and a teddy bear. The boy, who was at that time still the little boy, was watching a cartoon in the living room. I kissed his hair and closed myself in the bathroom again. When my husband came back, he sat on the machine and I peed three drops of pee. This time I didn't mess anything up. I lowered the toilet lid and put the test on it. I sat on the edge of the bathtub and waited, resting my head on my husband's legs, which were rocking gently with the damp, heavy, uterine, circular purr of the washing machine.

You're going to have a baby sister or brother, we announced to the little boy later that evening. He went on watching his cartoon.

I'd prefer a baby rabbit.

★

Salvatore gave me spaghetti for dinner. His apartment on the tenth floor of the building was full of books, cups, filing cabinets, useless things. They cried out for someone to impose a sense of narrative order. There was a bookcase crammed with LPs, but no longer anything to listen to them on. Salvatore pulled some out while he was cooking dinner. This one's a gem, he said, Roberto Murolo's early songs. I studied the track list, side A and side B: I didn't know any of them. You've got to hear this one, it's Neapolitan, too. And we'll have to listen to this one together some day. The small mountain of records went on growing – I piled them on the dining table. When the meal was ready, Salvatore put them back in their places. While we were eating, in what was perhaps a petty form of revenge, I talked to Salvatore about Latin American authors he hadn't read.

★

We're having sweet *tamales* for dinner. During the meal we first talk about the Hiroshima bombing, because the boy wants to know what an atomic bomb is, and then about the singer from Joy Division, whose name we can't remember. My husband embarks on a monologue about how he was one of the first people in the entire Spanish-speaking world to discover that band. We all nod and listen in silence. After a while, the boy interrupts him:

Can I say something too?

41

Yes.

I want to tell you both that I didn't see the end of *Raining Hamburgers* because I fell asleep.

★

The men I slept with used to fall asleep immediately after having sex, while I suffered insuperable sleeplessness, especially if the person had been able to give me pleasure. In that other city, in that apartment, I simply got out of bed and sat at my writing desk. I used to study Owen's portrait, which looked back at me like an apocryphal fruit from the autumn of yellow Post-its accumulating on the branches of the dead tree.

Owen had a distant, gloomy, spiritual face, like that of a religious martyr; high cheekbones, pointed chin, eyes disproportionately small. The body, languid, dispirited, submissive. Traces of Indian ancestry and an aristocratic *criollo* demeanor: none of the parts added up to the whole. I once read somewhere that personality is a continuous sequence of successful gestures. But the opposite was true of the man who appeared in the portrait: the fissures and discontinuities were obvious. Examining it closely, it was even easy to imagine the places where he'd attempted to cover a certain fragility with pieces of other personalities, firmer, more confident than his own.

★

My husband asks if it's true that I can't sleep after sex. I say:
Sometimes.
And what do you do when I fall asleep?
I hold you, listen to your breathing.
And then? he insists.
Then nothing, then I go to sleep.

★

During my second pregnancy, all I did was sleep. The contractions woke me up in the thirty-ninth week. My husband was reading beside me. I took his hand and placed it on the dome of my belly. Can you feel it? I asked. Is it kicking? No, it's coming. My first labor had to be induced and I ended up having a caesarean because I wasn't feeling anything, no contractions. This time, the sensation started in my lower back. An icy heat. Then, beginning in my sides, my skin raised itself up and tensed. A geological rather than biological phenomenon: a tremor, a slight arching, my entire belly rose up, like an emerging landmass, breaking through the surface of the sea. And the pain, a pain like a glint of light, the gleam of a comet, which leaves a trail, and fades away as incomprehensibly as it returns.

★

Note: Owen was born in El Rosario, Sinaloa. But that's not important. He was born on 4th February 1904. Or perhaps 13th May.

★

When I can't sleep, I go into my children's room and sit in the rocking chair. I listen to their slow breathing filling the whole room. The baby was also born on a 4th of February. The boy, on a 13th of May. Both were born on a Sunday.

★

I told Salvatore about the forgery. He had never heard of Gilberto Owen, but listened carefully to my rambling explanation. Owen had lived in Manhattan from 1928 through to 1930, at the height

43

of the Harlem Renaissance and the beginning of the Great Depression. Although Owen left letters, some diary entries and a handful of good poems, little is known of his period in New York. But it is known, I told Salvatore, that Owen lived in an old Harlem building opposite Morningside Park and that during those very years, on the other side of the park, Lorca was writing *Poet in New York*. A few blocks from there, Joshua Zvorsky was beginning his long poem *That*. Further north, Duke Ellington was playing in the Mexico Club. But Owen's writings from that time give the impression that he hated New York and was, in fact, on the margins of all that. It's most likely that he only came across Lorca once or twice, never met Zvorsky or saw Duke Ellington play.

So what? asked Salvatore.

So what what?

So what does it matter if he never met Lorca or saw Duke Ellington play?

It doesn't, I'm just saying he could have.

Exactly, and that's what matters.

★

The first installment of the sham transcription was a success. I arrived on Friday with a bundle of pages written in Word, 1.5 spacing, Times New Roman. White read them in front of me and was clearly interested, even enthusiastic. If they were indeed translations of poems by Owen made by Zvorsky, we'd found a treasure trove, I said. He replied that I was the best literary con-translator he'd ever met. Then he asked to see the original manuscript, which we both knew didn't exist.

I had to fabricate the manuscript over the weekend, with the help of Moby – he was the only person I knew with the tools and the talent to forge such a thing. He turned up at my apartment with a 1927 Remington and old paper. We worked all weekend. As a sort of reward, we made love on Sunday. He told me he liked my breasts, though they were a bit small. I said: Thank you.

★

Note: Owen died blind, victim of liver cirrhosis, on 9th March 1952, in Philadelphia. He'd swollen up so much that he'd grown breasts.

★

We have a neighbor who breeds frogs. And Madagascar cockroaches, to feed to the frogs. We meet him at the front door and the boy tells him that he has a dinosaur beside his bed, though it's made of foam rubber, because the hard plastic one got broken.

Live frogs are better, says the neighbor, because they eat the mosquitoes and cockroaches.

The boy looks at him steadily.

My dinosaur eats mosquitoes and frogs. But he doesn't eat cockroaches, he thinks they're disgusting.

★

I returned to Detective Matias's office many times. On my second visit, we had a coffee in the interrogation room while he asked me questions and I answered, convinced it was going to turn out that I was the guilty party. At that moment, looking Detective Matias in the eyes, I repented having stolen a calculator in my convent school at the age of eleven; I was assailed by the memory of the time a math teacher washed my mouth out with soap, arguing that I couldn't go home with such a dirty tongue; all the books I'd

45

stolen from so many libraries weighed on my conscience; the kisses I gave my girlfriend's boyfriend; the ones I gave my girlfriend. And then there was the forged collection of poems by Owen, translated by Zvorsky.

How many whiskies did you drink that night? he asked.

Less than one – perhaps a half, or three quarters of one.

How would you describe the individual who blocked your way when you were leaving the bar?

Medium build, not tall but not short either, darkish skin, maybe Hispanic.

Would you like to add anything?

No, thank you.

Detective Matias promised to call me when the case was solved. It would take a few weeks, perhaps months.

★

Our neighbor is preparing his forty-first birthday party. On Sunday he buys forty-one animals in the Sonora market and sets out boxes, fish tanks and cages in the courtyard before the astonished gazes of other neighbors arriving, slightly tipsy, from their family lunches. I watch them from the living-room window. The children admire the neighbor. He's going to liberate the animals on the day of his birthday, one animal for every year: three frogs, three turtles, two birds, thirty-two Madagascar cockroaches (*Gromphadorhina pertentosa*) and a wall lizard. All the neighbors are invited to the party. He tells a story about a trip to Thailand, a Buddhist ceremony, a temple, a woman, thirty-something animals, but I'm not listening. In the middle of the courtyard, two giant cockroaches are copulating inside a fish tank.

★

After the loan of the Remington, Moby felt free to come to my house more and more often. He'd spend whole days there, lying in my bathtub, cooking, watering the plants and drinking coffee with Dakota. I began to hate Moby. He smelt bad. He left horrible curly blonde hairs on my soap. I started borrowing Salvatore's armchair on the tenth floor, and returned home when I was certain Moby had left.

★

Yesterday my husband asked if he left hairs on the soap.

★

Years ago, I took a photo of Gilberto Owen. Or so I told Salvatore. It was the first time I told that lie. By now it's an elaborate lie, repeated to myself so often that it's come to form part of my repertory of events, indistinguishable from any other memory. Of course, I'd never seen Gilberto Owen, much less when he was young, and had certainly never taken a photo of him. But that's what I told Salvatore, not that he believed me. I was in a Lebanese café in Calle Donceles in the historic district of Mexico City, and Owen walked past under a huge black umbrella. It was a few minutes after five in the afternoon. There had just been one of those summer rainstorms, the likes of which only fall in Mexico City and Mumbai. The sidewalks were beginning to fill again with ambulant street vendors, tourists, cockroaches, and that sad peregrination of public servants hurrying back to their cubicles, suffused with satisfaction and guilt – their shirts wrinkled, their skin glinting with grease – after a short but sweet encounter in one of the pay-by-the-hour hotels in the zone. I told all that to Salvatore and then repented it. Describing Calle Donceles that way to a foreigner has an air of literary imposture I'm now

47

ashamed of. But Salvatore nodded, committed to my story, and, emboldened, I went on. I'd been in the Lebanese café for a few hours waiting for the rain to pass, half reading a scholarly edition of Rousseau's *Meditations*, half studying a group of old men drinking coffee and silently playing dominos at the next table. I'd got stuck on a Rousseauian phrase, possibly more ingenious than rational, about how adversity is a schoolmistress whose teaching comes too late to be truly useful. Salvatore remembered that meditation, he said. I had a Pentax with me that I'd just picked up from one of the camera repair shops on the street and, more from boredom than real interest, I'd been taking photos of the old men. Slow-witted pupils of adversity, Salvatore concluded, thinking himself very clever. When it finally stopped raining, I took a last gulp of coffee, put a twenty-peso bill under the sugar bowl and made my way to the door. (Passing the old men's table, I overheard them speculating about the firmness of my ass.) I stopped in the doorway for a moment to look along the street: rain-soaked, Mexico City returns to being that valley that obsessed Cortés, Juan Zorrilla and Velasco. I raised the camera, focused on a Rousseauian pedestrian who, at that moment, was jumping over a puddle, and shot.

★

Note (Owen writes): 'The public servant commonly suffers the abominable influence of the rain with Christian resignation and calmly prepares to edge his way meticulously from his home to the office, avoiding the mud and the potholes, doing balancing acts that make him sentimental and philosophical.'

★

Today I found Rousseau's *Meditations* on my husband's bedside table. He says he needs them for an article he's going to write for an urban-planning magazine. I can't imagine what relationship there might be between the two.

★

One night, Salvatore wanted to sleep with me. Do you know Inés Arredondo? I asked while he stroked one of my legs. Of course, he didn't. I'm going to give you her best story to read. It's called 'The Shunammite Woman'. It's about a young woman who goes to visit her uncle in the provinces. The uncle is dying and sends for her because he wants to bequeath her everything he owns. The young woman arrives in the town and her uncle immediately starts to improve. He forces her to marry him and to sleep in his sickbed. Thanks to the niece's vital presence, the uncle gets better by the day, until he's completely recovered. Salvatore caressed me; I, out of compassion, didn't stop him. That night, after dinner, I went back to my apartment. Before going to sleep, I cried a little and masturbated, looking at Owen's photo.

★

I took White the forged original. The truth is that with a little help from the villainous Moby, I had produced something worthy of being sold to an authentic collector. White promised to have an answer for me the following Monday and gave me the rest of the week off.

★

That bit about masturbating with a photo is disgusting, comments my husband. I'm annoyed, I defend myself like an insect and, so

49

as not to go on listening to his reproach, I read aloud from a pamphlet the neighbor who breeds frogs and Madagascar cockroaches gave us: 'When it is attacked or angered, the giant Madagascar cockroach flattens itself against the floor or ground and sharply expels the air in its respiratory passages, producing a disturbing snort, the aim of which is to frighten the aggressor.'

★

During my week off, Dakota and Moby were both staying in my apartment. I couldn't cope with the two of them at once, so on the Friday I decided to go to Philadelphia to visit Laura and Enea, and see if there might be an archive with documents about Owen in the Mexican consulate. The three of us had breakfast together and then I left. Moby would spend the entire weekend in his boxer shorts. Dakota would be occupying the bathtub the whole time. Perhaps, at some point on Saturday, Moby went into the bathroom and saw Dakota's clothes scattered on the floor, by the toilet. He saw a shapely calf and a foot, the nails painted. He apologized and went out, made himself a coffee or fried some eggs. Dakota would have come out a little later, wrapped in my towel. Maybe they had coffee together. They certainly made love in my bed and had breakfast together again on Sunday. Perhaps, some other Sunday, the three of us would have gotten into bed together.

★

On Sundays, my husband, the children and I listen to Rockdrigo and eat pancakes for breakfast. But not this Sunday. My husband is angry. Through my own carelessness, he's read some more of these pages. He asks how much is fiction and how much fact.

50

During that period, I took to telling lies. I lied more and more often, even in situations that didn't merit it. I suppose that's the logic of lies: one day you lay the first stone and the following day you have to lay two. When I was in Philadelphia, my sister took me to see a doctor because my left kidney – or perhaps ovary – was hurting. The consulate was closed the whole weekend, so all I did was walk with Laura and Enea, eat Chinese food, and then visit the doctor, having overdosed on monosodium glutamate. The receptionist handed me a form, which I filled in more or less like this:

Is this your first visit here? Yes.

Have you got a pain in your chest? Yes, it's really bad.

Are you unemployed? Yes.

What ethnic group do you belong to? Caucasian.

Do you belong to a church? Yes.

Which? Anglican.

Is there a history of cancer in your family? No.

What is your social security number? 12345.

★

Today was our neighbor's birthday: he didn't invite us to his party in the end.

★

The postman came by this morning. He hands me a postcard and I give him five pesos. It's from a woman in Philadelphia. It's for my husband. I read it. Perhaps, a few years ago, we'd have read it and laughed together; we'd have analyzed the exaggerated syntax of those who are selling some form of bygone happiness, then we'd have gotten drunk and made love in the kitchen, pretending for one night that we had no past. But we always choose – in some way it is our choice – to rehearse the beginnings of the end: beforeshocks, pre-tremblings.

★

When I got back from Philadelphia I immediately went to see White at the office. He wasn't there, but I found a long note stuck to my computer: 'You win. We'll publish a few poems in a magazine first. You can write an introductory note saying they're most probably by Z. But you still need to work on a lot of the poems. They're sloppy. When you're finished and the time's ripe, we'll bring out a book of the complete translations of O. Yours, White – PS Did you go to the cemetery in Philadelphia? I did some research and found out that Owen was buried there.'

★

Note (Postcard from Owen to Josefina Procopio, Philadelphia, 1950): '*Robin Hood Dell*. There's never before been an auditorium so completely open to the other world. The ghosts from Laurel Hill Cemetery, just behind the Dell, come to give concerts that other ghosts, from the great cemetery named Philadelphia, applaud. When it seems the Dell is full, they take a photograph and everything comes out empty because the film isn't sensitive to ghosts. I'm the shadow marked with an X.'

★

I suppose it's normal. The day comes when your husband's former lovers look at their legs, shed a few tears, put on fishnet stockings, and write a postcard to their first love. Some nights, when their own husband and children are sleeping, they put on an old record. Get modestly drunk. They write messages with overly complex, desperate grammar: discontinuous lines like varicose veins. The next morning they go to yoga classes and dye their hair bright red. Maybe, one day, they get a spider tattoo on their stomach. What's more likely is that this first love has been corresponding sporadically with them for years, so they feel free to write or call whenever and however they please and demand their share of lost youth, their drop-by-drop, prescribed dose of happiness. The men, if they're unhappy with their wife, will reply. The women, if they aren't yet ashamed of their body, will invite them to a hotel. Perhaps a hotel in Philadelphia.

★

I made an appointment with Detective Matias and went to see him at the police station. I haven't come to talk about the case, I said as I sat down in front of his desk – I'd been to see him so often that he no longer received me in the interrogation room. I've got a question for you, that's all. He listened.

What happens if someone publishes something, pretending someone else wrote it?

Like a literary ghostwriter?

More or less.

I don't know. I don't read much. But last Christmas my daughter gave me *The Maltese Falcon*. Have you read it?

★

My husband and I have been asked to a dinner party with old friends. I go into the bathroom to do my face before leaving. I put on eyeliner, mascara, and brush my teeth. I've got dark shadows under my eyes. We turn off the gas, shut the windows and doors overlooking the inner patio. We switch off all the lights, except the one in the hall. We say goodnight to the children and the babysitter. I take his arm when we're outside and he tells me that, before we left, he killed a Madagascar cockroach by the baby's cot. Then he quickly says: I may have to go to Philadelphia to oversee the construction. I drop his arm and say I have to check the baby one more time, that the cockroach thing terrifies me. I go inside and turn on the lights. My husband follows me. I open the gas tap and the door to the inner patio. I don't want to go out, don't want to go to a dinner party. I go into the children's room and the creak of the door wakes the baby. She cries, I have to pick her up. I can't go with you, I say, you go alone.

★

Leave a life. Blow everything up. No, not everything: blow up the square meter you occupy among people. Or better still: leave empty chairs at the tables you once shared with friends, not metaphorically, but really, leave a chair, become a gap for your friends, allow the circle of silence around you to swell and fill with speculation. What few people understand is that you leave one life to start another.

★

Note: From 1928 to 1929, Owen had an unimportant job in the Mexican consulate in New York. During that time, he wrote an article entitled 'Production-line system for shelling, cleaning and grading peanuts'.

★

The boy talks to the ghost in our house. He tells me so while we're bathing the baby together. He pours water on her head with a sponge while I clean her whole body with neutral soap. We know we're handling something very fragile. Folds and folds of delicate flesh.

D'you know what?

What?

Without doesn't scare me any more.

That's good.

Don't you worry, Mama, Without's going to look after us when Papa goes to Philadelphia.

Why do you think Papa's going to Philadelphia?

But where is Philadelphia?

★

A selection of the forged poems was published in a small but prestigious magazine and afterwards, thanks to the kudos conferred by the name of Zvorsky, came the shower of mentions an author needs to find a place in the market: reviews. First on obscure Internet sites specializing in third-world authors, translations, and minority writers in general (ethnic, racial, sexual, et cetera). Later, articles appeared in academic journals, attesting to the authenticity of the 'manuscript containing translations by the poet Zvorsky of the great Mexican poet Gilberto Owen, found in the Casa Hispánica of Columbia University'. The Department of Hispanic Literature at the University of Austin opened an 'Owen Archive'; the articles Owen had written for *El Tiempo* in Bogotá in the 1930s and 1940s appeared, edited by a university professor and issued by a well-known publishing house in Mexico City, and were immediately translated for Harvard University Press. A hail of apocryphal manuscripts, all related to Owen's sojourn in New York, appeared. A 'lost' issue of the magazine *Exile*, edited by

Ezra Pound, came to light, with extracts from *Línea*, the collection of poems Owen published around 1930. Our plans were going well. I'd keep working on the rest of the poems and we would have a book ready in a few months.

★

The design for the Philadelphia house is, finally, almost finished. My husband left the plans on his desk and now it's me who's looking for something. I rummage. On some of the plans there are two figures, a man and a woman roughly sketched in pencil, who live in that house. They're eating in the kitchen, taking a bath together in an enormous tub, sleeping in a room with a huge window.

I log on to his computer to see if I can find another clue there. The program he uses is called AutoCAD. I open it, press keys, more and more windows open, a whole house, in three dimensions, spacey, with white wooden doors. There are labels where there will eventually be chairs, bookshelves, plants and pictures. But I do not find him there, or her.

★

Dakota moved to her new house at the beginning of summer. It was an apartment in Queens, near a cemetery. The day they handed over the keys we went out to buy three cans of paint. She wanted her whole house to look like Juliet Berto's cobalt-blue bathroom in *Céline et Julie vont en bâteau*. We opened all the windows and stripped down to our panties. We painted the bathroom, the kitchen, but only half of the bedroom because we ran out of paint. We painted each other's nipples cobalt blue. When we'd finished we lay face up on the bedroom floor and lit a cigarette apiece. Dakota suggested we swap panties.

Note (Owen to Salvador Novo, Philadelphia, 1949): 'Here, in summer, women develop miniature Mount Etnas they call breasts; they're very unsettling things that sometimes turn out to be what are called "cheaters", which can be bought in any women's fashion store.'

★

For the last few days there have been workmen in the house across the street. They're taking up the old floorboards and re-placing them with parquet. They listen to the radio the whole day. That's how I find out what's happening in the outside world. There was an earthquake in Asia; sham elections in Nepal; the Mexican army found a mass grave in Tamaulipas with the bodies of seventy-two undocumented Central American migrants. The workmen have sussed out what time I breastfeed the baby, in a rocking chair by the window. They watch me from the roof, lined up like recruits, candidates for a feast to which they won't be invited. I close the blinds and unbutton my blouse.

★

In the mornings, my husband continues to read what I've writ-ten the night before. It's all fiction, I tell him, but he doesn't believe me.

Weren't you writing a novel about Owen?

Yes, I say, it's a book about Gilberto Owen's ghost.

★

Note (Owen to Josefina Procopio, Philadelphia, 1948): 'As this month the 4th was a Sunday, logically tomorrow will be Tuesday the 13th and

I'm to die on a Tuesday the 13th. But if tomorrow isn't the day, Death will wait for me, or I for her, the appointment won't be this year. Let's see what happens.'

★

In *One Thousand and One Nights* the narrator strings together a series of tales to put off the day of her death. Perhaps a similar but reverse mechanism would work for this story, this death. The narrator discovers that while she is stringing the tale, the mesh of her immediate reality wears thin and breaks. The fiber of fiction begins to modify reality and not vice versa, as it should be. Neither of the two can be sacrificed. The only remedy, the only way to save all the planes of the story, is to close one curtain and open another: lower one blind so you can unbutton your blouse; un-write a story in one file and construct a different plot in another. Change the characters' names, remember that everything is or should be fiction. Write what really did happen and what did not. At the end of each day's work, separate the paragraphs, copy, paste, save; leave only one of the files open so the husband reads it and sates his curiosity to the full. The novel, the other one, is called *Philadelphia*.

★

This is how it starts: it all happened in another city and another life. It was the summer of 1928. I was working as a clerk in the Mexican consulate in New York, writing official reports on the price of Mexican peanuts on the US market, which was about to crash. Almost twenty-five years have gone by since then; even if I wanted to, I couldn't write this story as if I still lived there and were that thin young man, full of enthusiasm, translating Dickinson and Williams, wrapped in a gray bathrobe.

(I would have liked to start the way Fitzgerald's *The Crack-up* begins.)

★

My husband has a future life in Philadelphia I know nothing about. A story that perhaps unfolds on the back of his plans. I don't want to know anything more about it. I'm tortured, irremediably, *a priori*, by pieces of a life already traced out but not lived, in which there's a woman, in a house without children, a self-confident *criolla*, who moans when she fucks. My husband sketches it all out and believes I don't know.

★

The children live with my ex-wife in New York. I have an apartment and a grave in Philadelphia. She's a *criolla* who vamps *criollos*. Fair-skinned, wealthy. She comes from an old established Colombian family. I never belonged in that world. My father was an Irish miner who didn't bequeath me his red hair but did pass on his sense of class resentment and a talent for debauchery. We met in Bogotá, and married there. We had two morganatic children and were, like almost everyone else, unhappy – 'largely unhappy', as the Yankees would elegantly put it. A few years ago we both did a '*criollazo*'. I lost everything in a Bogotá gaming house. She went off to Manhattan to start a career as a resentful poet. I came to Philadelphia, though I'm not quite sure what I intended to start.

Criollazo: the act of leaving one's husband in one's prime, before hitting forty, to dedicate oneself to other women's husbands. *Criollazo*: the act of leaving one's wife, on the threshold of fifty, to dedicate oneself to women without husbands.

59

★

The problem with *criollos*, and even more so with *criollas*, is that they're convinced they deserve a better life than the one they have. (Note how often a *criolla* uses the word 'deserve' in any conversation with another *criolla*). They firmly believe that inside their head is a diamond someone should discover, polish and put on a red cushion, so that everyone can be amazed, marvel, understand what they have been missing.

★

I've been living in Philadelphia for three years. After a bit of string-pulling in the Foreign Ministry, which I'd prefer not to linger on, I managed to be appointed honorary consul here. It was the only way I had of living near the children. But none of that matters now: I'm going blind, I'm fat, so fat I've got tits, sometimes I tremble, perhaps stutter. I've got three cats and I'm going to die.

★

The subway, its multiple stops, its breakdowns, its sudden accelerations, its dark zones, could function as the space-time scheme for this other novel.

★

Every fortnight I go to Manhattan to visit the children. Returning, a couple of decades on, to that city where I died so many times has something of a pilgrimage to the cemetery about it, except that instead of taking flowers to a relative or grieving at the grave of an unknown child, I go to meet the men and women I never was but, at the same time, have never been able to stop being.

★

The subway used to bring me close to dead things; to the death of things. One day, when I was traveling home from the south of the city on the 1 line, I saw Owen again. This time it was different. This time it wasn't an external impression caused by something outside me, like that night in the bar in Harlem, nor a fleeting impression like the time before in the subway, but the stabbing certainty that I was in the presence of something at once beautiful and terrible. I was looking out of the window – nothing except the heavy darkness of the tunnels – when another train approached from behind and for a few moments traveled at the same speed as the one I was on. I saw him sitting in the same position as me, his head resting against the carriage window. And then nothing. His train speeded up and many other bodies, smudged and ghostly, passed before my eyes. When there was once again darkness outside the window, I saw my own blurred image on the glass. But it wasn't my face; it was my face superimposed on his – as if his reflection had been stamped onto the glass and now I was reflected inside that double trapped on my carriage window.

★

A horizontal novel, told vertically. A novel which has to be told from the outside in order to be read from within.

★

Naturally, there are a lot of deaths in the course of a lifetime. Most people don't notice. They think you die once and that's it.

But you only have to pay a bit of attention to realize that you go and die every so often. That's not just a poetic turn of phrase. I'm not saying the soul this and the soul that, but that one day you cross the street and a car knocks you down; another day you fall asleep in the bathtub and never get out; and another, you tumble down the stairs of your building and crack your head open. Most deaths don't matter: the film goes on running. Except that that's when everything takes a turn, even though it may be imperceptible, and the consequences are not always apparent straight away.

I began to die in Manhattan, in the summer of 1928. Of course, no one except me noticed my deaths – people are too busy with their own lives to take note of other people's little deaths. I noticed because after each death I got a temperature and lost weight.

I used to weigh myself every morning, to see if I'd died the day before. And though it didn't happen all that often, I was losing pounds at an alarming rate (I never knew how much it was in kilos). It's not that I got any thinner. I just lost weight, as if I were hollowing out, while my shell remained intact. Now, for instance, I'm fat and have man boobs, but I scarcely weigh three pounds. I don't know if that means I've got three deaths left, as if I were a cat counting backwards. No, I don't think so. I think the next one will be the real thing.

★

Dakota and I visited the cemetery near her house in Queens. We went to leave a bunch of flowers for Lucky Luciano, a mafioso to whom she claimed to be distantly related. Luciano had been stabbed in the face in 1929, and was left with a squint in one eye. Dakota described the scene to me with almost literary precision as we were making our way down the long cemetery paths lined with photographs and white lilies. Three men had forced him into a limo at gunpoint and destroyed his face with a knife, but made sure he was still alive. They dumped him on a beach on Long Island. Lucky Luciano walked to the nearest hospital, covering the socket of his injured eye with his hand. The story seemed to me more hilarious than tragic, despite all Dakota's efforts to move me. After searching for his grave for a while, we came across Robert Mapplethorpe's. Dakota had an attack of mock nostalgia and wanted to stop for a moment. She requested silence. I'd never liked Mapplethorpe's photos, but I condescended to sit with her in the sun, one on either side of the gravestone, like two premature effigies of Patti Smith. After a few minutes a white cat appeared from among the bushes and prostrated itself in Dakota's lap. That seemed to her a sign of something, and perhaps she was right. She wanted to take it home. I tried to dissuade her, because cemetery cats never get used to the company of the living, but Dakota took no notice. We left Mapplethorpe the flowers we'd brought for poor old Lucky Luciano and went to buy cat food.

★

Salvatore was having a party. Come with your friends, he said. He was in an over-excited, celebratory mood, preparing for his seventieth birthday. He reviewed the menu with me, over and over: pork stuffed with pomegranate seeds, salad with cashew nuts and goat's cheese, white rice with coconut milk. I brought Dakota, who brought the new cat and her ex-boyfriend; I brought Moby and Pajarote; I called White, who didn't turn up; I brought Salvatore back his record player. His friends also arrived, in a painfully slow trickle. A woman who'd been a ballerina and was still displaying her collarbones and pulling in her abs, as if this would heal the blow of so many years without leotards and tutus;

an elderly entomologist who mated fruit flies in a laboratory; a young girl, Salvatore's student, who was trying to score points with the birthday boy.

We ate around an oak coffee table, covered in papers, in the center of the living room. We listened to records while gently touching legs and shoulders, lounging on the couch or the floor, generating false hopes of the degenerate orgy that never occurred. Salvatore talked for hours about the erection of a young Neapolitan guy he'd seen on a nudist beach when he was seventeen. While we were chewing pieces of pork, he made some reference to a movie by a Portuguese director, whose name I can never remember, in which someone is nibbling a pomegranate. Apparently, it was an erotic scene. One of the guests threw up in the kitchen. Dakota's cat ate the vomit. The entomologist took the baton, speculating about the relationship between the quantity of sugar in the fruit and the reproductive cycles of the flies. Salvatore's student sat on the back of the armchair, behind him, and demonstrated the principal points of Thai massage while commenting on how sad it was that the Australian shark was in imminent danger of extinction. Pajarote fell asleep on Dakota's lap. She was singing something by Bessie Smith and stroking the head of her ex-boyfriend, who was sitting on the floor, rubbing his foot against mine while leafing through the papers Salvatore had laid out on the table in staged disorder, specially for that night, the night of his birthday.

Anyone for coffee? asked the birthday boy, after a long silence.

Several hands were raised.

Salvatore left the living room and didn't return. He'd fallen, exhausted, onto his bed. Before leaving, we all filed into his room. His student kissed his forehead and we emulated her, as if it were a funeral. Then, everyone left at the same instant, like the ghostly members of a hypothetical *corps de ballet*. Moby and I stayed on. We tried making love in Salvatore's armchair, he touched my breasts. I wanted to kiss him, but his neck smelled of pomegranate and pork and I had to go to the bathroom to throw up. When I came back, Moby had gone. That was the last time I saw him.

★

I've stopped breastfeeding the baby. Five days with my boobs hard and red. But the thought of not producing milk is heartening. It wasn't easy, it's never easy, being a person who produces milk.

★

When Moby disappeared, Pajarote began to come on Wednesdays again. We breakfasted on toast with cheese and honey; I drank coffee with cream, Pajarote had a can of Coca-Cola. He explained some theories about the degree of semantic opacity and conventionality of metaphors. He was writing a paper on judgments and their semantic relationship to a word associated with the literal and figurative meanings of utterances. I preferred the cat theory. Pajarote used to talk with his mouth full of toast. The crumbs fell on the table and kitchen floor. When he'd gone, I furiously vacuumed the apartment.

★

Both toilets in the house are blocked. The downstairs one went first. It overflows if you pull the chain. Shit flows out all over the place. My husband unblocks it, swabs the bathtub with bleach, mops the floor frenetically. No use. Next it's the upstairs one. Same problem. The boy says it's the neighbor's cockroaches blocking the pipes.

65

★

The literal and figurative meanings of utterances: Salvatore wasn't a biologist, he was a professor of biology.

★

Detective Matias didn't contact me again for several months. But, finally, he called. We've closed the case, he announced over the phone, I've been transferred to a different precinct. He personally apologized for not having gotten anywhere. The truth is that I'd stopped caring about the case, and simply liked visiting him once in a while, asking him questions, listening to his answers. I went to see him one last time in his office on 126th Street. He offered me coffee and talked about growing up as an Ecuadorian kid in the Bronx. He unashamedly hated blacks. When he was a boy, two Afro-Americans cracked his skull open in the schoolyard because he couldn't get the ball in the basket. They beat me up and pulled down my shorts and my underpants. They saw my little ass, *mi culito*, he said, using Spanish for the first time.

★

The 1 line runs the length of Manhattan. It starts at the ferry terminal at the southern tip of the island, goes through part of Chelsea and up to Columbia University on 116th Street, where Owen used to take the train every day to the south of the city, after weighing himself on a machine by the ticket office. The line continues up to Harlem and I don't know how much further. The track goes on and on, beyond the island, beyond this story.

★

My husband announces at breakfast that he'll be going to Phila-delphia soon, and doesn't know how long he'll be away. Have you got a workery in Philadelphia? asks the boy. My husband ignores him and goes on talking. Papa, Papa, the boy insists, have you got a Philadelphia cheese workery, Papa?

Pa-pa, says the baby.

★

Philadelphia is falling down. And so is this apartment. Too many things, too many voices. There are three cats that appeared out of the blue one day. And a ghost, or several ghosts, also appeared. I can't see the ghosts, nor can I make out the cats very clearly, but in my world of white shadows they're one more obstacle to bump into every day – like the writing desk, the Reposet chair in which I used to read, the doors left ajar.

Of course, my blindness wasn't instantaneous, and neither was the appearance of all these new tenants. But the day those things began to arrive – the blindness, the cats, the ghosts, the pieces of furniture and dozens of books I hadn't bought, and, of course, later on, the flies and the cockroaches – I knew it was the begin-ning of the end. Not mine, but the end of something I had iden-tified with so closely that it would soon do away with me too.

If eyes can be compared with reflective pools of water, then the punishment of terminal blindness falls on them like a cataract. Blindness, like castigation and cataracts, comes from above, with no obvious purpose or meaning; and it's accepted with the hum-ble resignation of a body of water trapped in a pool, perpetually fed by more of itself. My blindness is black and white and I have a veritable Niagara on my brow.

★

Finally there came the day White had been waiting for so eagerly. For months, I had worked hard on the poems, and the book was scheduled to go to print in a couple of weeks. We were going to publish another selection of poems in advance of the book, this time in the *New York Review of Books*, and a renowned critic had asked to interview White and myself for a full profile of the poet Gilberto Owen, his years in New York, and his relationship to Zvorsky. We booked an appointment with him for the following week.

White invited me to raise a glass for Owen and cut down his tree. He'd finally made up his mind to do it. We'd use an electric saw, connected by an extension lead to a socket in his apartment. We had two pairs of thick, leather gloves. Wellingtons. A bottle of whisky. Aplomb.

But the saw didn't work, so we ordered pizza and sat on the steps outside his building. White talked about his wife, how difficult the first years without her had been, the impossibility of throwing out her clothes, her books, her toiletries. White was an inconsolable man. He'd decided to set up the publishing house because the project had been her idea.

Why did you hire me, White? I asked after taking a long swig from the bottle.

Because, the day I interviewed you, I realized you smoked the same brand of tobacco as her. It was a way of smelling her every day. But, what the heck, let's talk about Owen and Zvorsky. Maybe we can plan an anthology of Latin American poets translated by false William Carlos Williamses and Pounds.

I'd been stung, I realized a few hours or perhaps a few days later, to understand that White had never believed in me. Or Owen. If he'd hired me, it was because I smelled a bit like his wife. If we were going to publish Owen, it was because White wanted to publish Zvorsky, albeit apocryphally. I was just a whiff, a trail, a puff of smoke.

★

I suppose that's what illness is like: you stand down and are replaced by the ghost of yourself. But at the same time, illness, and maybe particularly one like mine, which expresses itself in blindness, allows the sufferer to observe himself, as he would the picturesque, headlong descent of a cataract – from afar, without getting soaked, alarmed but not *touched* by the experience. Everything that had begun to happen to me since my arrival in Philadelphia – my constantly expanding body, my face disappearing before me in the mirror, the shadows of things replacing the things-in-themselves – started happening to that other person, the ghost of me, the poor idiot trapped under the constant rush of a cataract.

★

All novels lack something or someone. In that novel there's no one. No one except a ghost that I used to see sometimes in the subway.

★

I used to check my weight every day in the subway station on 116th Street. It was always less, I was disappearing slowly inside my little unloved bureaucrat's suit, but I wrote to a very pretty girl to say that I was filling out, that I was now a man, nearly, that she should give in and marry me. I lied: 125 pounds, 126 pounds. Beloved Clementina, sweet Dionisia, my letters began. At heart, even I didn't believe anything I wrote, but I liked the idea of being a despairing poet in New York. I was leading an imbecilic life, but I liked it. I kept an almost metaphysical distance from things and people, but I liked it. I felt ghostly, and I liked that most of all. I didn't know that I was one of those people with a talent for creating 'self-fulfilling prophecies', as the Yankees say. I didn't know that, with time, I would really become a ghost. I was twenty-something, I allowed myself the luxury of writing about my thin body, of masturbating in the window, wrapped in a gray silk bathrobe, gray as my Harlem youth, dull as all youths in neighborhoods with literary names.

★

Not a fragmented novel. A horizontal novel, narrated vertically.

★

Three or four days after my conversation with White, I got an invitation from some institute or other that organized tributes to Mexican artists based in Brooklyn. From the outset, I knew the sort of nightmare I'd be getting into if I decided to go. It seemed to me, even then, and I believe rightly, that those events were just a modern-day version of Latin-American civilized barbarity. The only difference being that now there was no contemporary Rubén Darío to write a redemptive column justly pillorying the participants.

I asked Pajarote to go with me. We'll be rubbing shoulders with *criollo* trustafarians! he said – and for a moment I didn't know if this was said with eagerness or sarcasm. Pajarote explained that 'trustafarians' were wage earners, like us, except the wage came from their parents. In New York they lived a Bohemian life, but in Mexico they had uniformed maids. They snorted cocaine but were vegetarians, vegans or even freegans. They dressed like teenagers – in T-shirts saying 'Brooklyn' and 'Mind the Gap' – but the guys didn't have much hair and the women had premature crow's feet.

We hired period costumes from some place in SoHo – to tell

the truth, I don't know if they were from the twenties or the fifties or a cobbled-together mix of the two – and drove to Brooklyn. We arrived arm in arm, seething with middle-class resentment. We were offered a shot of mescal and a bag of sherbet candies called Space Dust: Green or orange? asked a good-looker in hotpants, wearing a nametag that said 'Fani' and a false moustache *à la* Frida Kahlo. We both chose green then mingled with our trustafarian compatriots.

I wanted to talk to Pajarote. He was the only person with moral intelligence I knew in the city, the only one who would tell me if I should go ahead with my publication plans. I wasn't morally encumbered. I was afraid. And angry with White. More than anything, I'd lost any sense of purpose. But that night Pajarote had left his intelligence at home. He immediately Space Dusted Fani: he was wearing outsized fake glasses with heavy frames, and was feeling very self-confident. Although he in fact looked a bit like a Latino version of the young Zvorsky, he was convinced he resembled a London rock star – languid, indifferent. I went on drinking mescal, pretty much alone, diligently standing before all the pictures and installations in the venue (a loft). I was looking at a series representing a woman's veined feet when I was cornered by a small bald man who could have been interesting if he'd tried a little less hard.

These gimcrack paintings are mine.

Who do all the feet belong to?

My ex-wives.

Sorry.

No pro... Do you have a card?

(That's what he said: 'pro'.)

No.

The young lady has no card!

(He was one of those people who speak with exclamation marks.)

Here's mine… If you'll let me… I'll paint you something…
(He was one of those people who speak with dot-dot-dots.)
Thanks.
What's your name? he asked.
Owen.
Isn't that a man's name?
Could be.
I'd like to see your feet…
My what?
Baldy invited me to his own loft (upper-class Mexicans pronounce it *laaaft*). I'm an artist, he said, I live right here in Brooklyn – as if saying artist and Brooklyn in the same breath was to create a self-sustainable world. We took a cab for which he, naturally, paid. Before leaving, I said goodnight to Pajarote, ashamed, beaten, humiliated, and feeling that in some way it was his fault that I was going home with a trustafarian. I got into the cab, took off my shoes and settled my bare feet in Baldy's crotch.

★

I think that when I was young I was weighed down by a constant sense of social inadequacy – I was never the most popular nor the most eloquent at a table; never the best read nor the best writer; not the most successful nor the most talented; definitely not the most handsome nor the one who had most luck with women. At the same time, I harbored the secret hope, or rather, the secret certainty, that one day I would finally turn into myself; into the image of myself I'd been elaborating for years. But when I now reread the notes or poems I wrote then, or when I recall the conversations with other members of my generation, and the ideas we so boldly expounded, I realize that the truth is I've been getting more imbecilic by the day. I've spent too many years sleeping, dozing. I don't know at what moment an inversion began to occur in the process that I imagined as linear and ascending, and which, in the end, turned out to be a sort of pitiless boomerang that flies back and knocks out your teeth, your enthusiasm and your balls.

★

The boy asks:
    Do you know what's under the house?
    What?
    Little balls.
    And what else?
    Little dots, about fifty-six little dots.
    And on top of the house?
    On top there's a man having a little sleep.

★

When I was in other people's beds, I slept deeply and got up early the next morning. I'd dress quickly, steal the odd personal item – my favorites were towels, which smelt good, or white singlets – and depart in a good mood. I'd buy a coffee to go, a newspaper, and sit in some very public space, in full sunlight, to read. What I most liked about sleeping in other people's beds was precisely that, waking up early, rushing out, buying a real newspaper, and reading in the sun.

★

My husband stands behind me as I write. He massages my shoulders, too hard, and reads what's on the screen.
    Is it him saying that or you?

73

Him – she barely speaks now.

And what about you, how many men have you slept with?

Only four, or perhaps five.

And now?

No one else. What about you?

★

Note (Owen to Villaurrutia): 'I'm not in love. She's Swedish. And I had her as a virgin, a mystical experience I can recommend. She's got a cold passion. She throws herself at me like a Hindu woman onto the pyre on which the body of her prince consort burns. And as she gets up before me, I'm never sure if I didn't go to bed with an ice sculpture that has melted.'

★

I spent four days and three nights hiding, I don't know from whom or from what, in Baldy's house. The first night he couldn't get it up. The second day, he went out before I woke up and didn't return that night. I called Pajarote to see how things had gone with Fani, the hostess, but no one answered the phone. When it was clear that the owner of the apartment wasn't coming back that day, I rang Dakota and invited her to spend the night with me. She came round at about ten and we watched *Pet Sematary* projected onto an enormous white wall. We ate cans of smoked oysters and had a bath together in a tub filled with cartoon characters of the 1990s: there was Ursula, the octopus woman, the hyena from *The Lion King*, Aladdin, one of the fat fairy godmothers from *Sleeping Beauty*, and a philosophical Smurf. Dakota sang all the bits of the songs she could remember. When I could, I helped out with the backing vocals. When we got out of the bathtub, wrinkly, we dried each other using immense towels with Baldy's initials embroidered in gold thread, and Dakota asked me to put cream on her back. We anointed each other and put on a DVD of a television series starring a blond guy who invariably saved the world.

The third day, Baldy turned up in stud mode with a box of oil paints, assorted bottles of liquor, condoms and hard drugs. Dakota and I were comfortably ensconced on his leather sofa, watching the blond guy's courageous efforts to save New York from a germ bomb. He offered us a martini; we accepted on condition we could finish watching the whole DVD. He gave us a lecture on the episodic nature of series and their relationship to the structure of *Don Quijote*. He was an intelligent but complicated man. Owen would have said that he spoke with spelling mistakes. He offered us Colombian cocaine, and took five hundred photos of our feet with a digital camera while the blond guy was torturing three Moslems with one hand.

By the time the DVD finished, the sun was already coming up. Dakota and Baldy had moved to the bed. I rushed out. I got a coffee in the street, bought a newspaper and started walking to the subway – I had an appointment with White the next day.

Dakota kept Baldy, as she had kept Moby, and all my other leftovers. She was like a lobster; and I, like the filth that accumulates on the seabed.

In the subway, on my way home, I saw Owen for the last time. I believe he waved to me. But by then it didn't matter, I'd lost my enthusiasm. Something had broken. The ghost, it was obvious, was me.

★

I suppose that the difference between being young and being old is the degree of frivolity in our relationship with death. When I was young, my disdain for life was such that I was constantly imagining ever more extravagant deaths. It's Sod's Law that now, when I'd prefer to be simply alive and spend time with my kids, I'm suffering a slow, humiliating, boring death, through no fault but my own. My deaths in Manhattan were quick and had external causes: a subway train cracked my skull open; a man buried a knife in my chest when I was leaving a bar; my appendix burst at midnight; I allowed myself to fall to the ground from the top floor of a Financial District building. But death in Philadelphia is approaching like a bedraggled cat, it rubs its dirty ass up against my lower leg, licks my hands, scratches my face, asks me for food; and I feed it.

★

I called Pajarote late on Sunday night. I told him about White and Owen, said that I was going to see White the following day. I told him about Baldy and Dakota. He listened.

Imagine a series of men, he said. The first of them has a full head of hair and the last is completely bald. Each successive member of the series has a single hair less than the one before. It would appear that the three following statements are true:

1. The first man in the series is not bald.
2. If a man is not bald, a single hair less will not make him bald.
3. The last man in the series is bald.

And so what?
That's the Sorites paradox.
What?
The paradox is that, although those three statements appear to be true, in conjunction they involve a contradiction.

And what am I supposed to do with that?

Nothing, understand it.

★

On the day of the interview I got to the office early, carrying the wooden chair I'd stolen almost a year before. White and I had decided to meet up a few hours before the interview to go over the details of our story, from that first letter with the address of Owen's old apartment in Harlem, to the notes and Zvorsky's translations. White was like a child, more excited than I'd ever seen him. I even thought that the shadow which had been darkening his brow for months or years had disappeared. He wanted to tell the critic about the episode in the bar, when I'd hallucinated Owen eating the remains of Pound's peanuts while Zvorsky conducted an imaginary orchestra. White was saying this when I cut him short.

I'm not going to do it.

What?

You know I translated those poems by Owen, not Zvorsky.

Huh? Are you trying to tell me you want your name on the book? he asked, as if not wishing to understand.

No, I'm telling you I'm not going to do it.

White's upper lip trembled slightly, he didn't say a word.

★

Note: Owen went to Detroit a few days after Black Tuesday, when the Great Depression began.

★

My husband is packing. They're going to start building the house in Philadelphia. I'm not really sure why an architect has to be there the whole time during the construction of a house for which he's already drawn up the plans. But he insists that's the way it's done, that the architect always has to be present on site. The baby wakes up at midnight. She cries. She needs a bottle.

★

Baldy fell for Dakota. She fell for his bathtub. They began a tortuous, dangerous, multilateral relationship.

I received my last paycheck in the mail, with an absurd little note from Minni: Thanks for smiling.

I was going to leave New York as soon as possible.

★

When are you going to Philadelphia?

Next week, next month, I don't know, as soon as possible.

So why are you packing now?

Because that's what you just wrote. You left your document open while you were feeding the baby and I read a bit.

But it's only a novel, none of it exists.

★

Moby existed. But he wasn't called Moby. His name was Bobby. When I found out – Dakota told me – I was shaken by a fit of giggles, and then tears. But Bobby's not important, because he perhaps doesn't exist any longer.

The boy and the baby exist. A house exists, the creaking of the old floorboards, the internal shuddering of the things we own, the palimpsestic windows that hold the impressions of hands and lips. My husband and I exist, though our existence is increasingly

78

separate, and the neighbors, the neighborhood and the cockroaches that pass silently by also exist.

★

You're a liar, he says.
  Why?
  You're a liar.
  So are you.

★

Follow the line of a story, like the line of the ass of an Ecuadorian child who was later a detective in Harlem. Crack heads with everyone, fight everything, the past, the present, so long as the story moves on. Never stray from the line. Close your eyes, put the bucket over your head and sing, just to imagine that flat, firm, dark *culito*.

★

I gave away my furniture and shared all the plants – except for the dead tree – among my acquaintances. I caught the train to Philadelphia. I wanted to leave the dead tree in the cemetery there. Laura and Enea took me, they didn't ask questions: they're the kind of people who know how to respect others, not to ask for explanations. We went to the cemetery but never found Owen's grave. They offered to keep the plant. We're still watering it even though we know it's dead, they tell me now, when we speak on the phone. The pot is by their front door. Their neighbors, born-again Christians, ask about the dead plant. They have gardenias in the entrance. They're born-again people who ask for explanations and have gardenias. That's what Laura and Enea tell me when we

79

speak on the phone and I ask how the plant is doing: The neighbors hate it, you know, they're newborn Christians, they have gardenias perpetually in flower on the porch.

★

My husband is going to Philadelphia tomorrow. He's in the kitchen making dinner for us all. The boy sits down at the kitchen table to draw. I can hear them from the living room:

Look, Papa, I've made a house to live in.

Uhuh.

Do you know what happened to my house?

What?

A gyranium wind came and gobbled it up.

You don't say gyranium, you say twister.

A twister wind came and gobbled it up.

Not twister wind, just twister.

I like gyrawind twister.

★

The day I bought a plane ticket out of New York, I tried to speak to White on the telephone. Almost a month had gone by since the last time I'd seen him, and I at least wanted to say I was leaving the city for good. Minni answered: He says he can't talk to you now, but not to worry, I don't know what he meant, you know how he is, but he told me to tell you not to worry. He says you might want to read the next issue of the NYRB.

★

My husband went to Philadelphia today. I suppose it was to be expected. Months and years had piled one on top of the other for this moment to arrive. First, the mutual persecution. Hounding one another until neither has a centimeter of air. Conceiving an infinite hatred of the other. Not so much boredom (that would have been to remain at his side for twenty years and end up sleeping in separate beds). Not so much the contempt (the inadequate size of his hands, the smell of his sleeping body, the taste of his sex). But the hatred. Breaking him, emotionally decimating him again and again. Allowing oneself to be broken. Writing this is coarse. But reality is even more so. Later, the moral accusations. The list of the defects of the accused, always accompanied by the tacit list of the virtues of the accuser. Our final hours together were predictable: the temperature of the arguments rising, the almost comic melodrama of the play beginning. Faces, masks. One shouting, the other crying; and then, change masks. For one, two, three, six hours, until the world finally falls apart: tomorrow, this Sunday, next Wednesday, Christmas. But in the end, a strange peace, gathered from who knows what rotten gut. It was a single gesture that broke me – that finished breaking me: his cry of joy when he had closed the front door.

★

Dakota wanted to organize a going-away party for me. We decided to hold it in the empty apartment. Her ex-boyfriend came, and some of the rotating members of the band. Pajarote came with Fani. We didn't invite Moby alias Bobby. Baldy turned up with his ex-wife – a slightly silly Mexican *criolla* who had put herself through a master's at NYU only to end up teaching Spanish in a Brooklyn secondary school; and she brought her new partner, another Mexican *criolla* who repeatedly quoted lyrics by Joaquín Sabina. And that was all.

In the kitchen, Dakota's ex-boyfriend asked me why I was just up and leaving like that. I told him that I'd turned into a ghost; or maybe that I was the only living girl in a city of ghosts; that, in any case, I didn't like dying all the time. He stroked my forehead. I didn't know what to do. Spontaneous gestures paralyze me. Perhaps I could have touched his face; licked the naked scar that furrowed it into two possible faces. I could have told him that I was going because I was incapable of sustaining and inhabiting the worlds I myself had fabricated, that I also had a scar splitting my face in two. Perhaps I could have made love to him in the bathtub. Perhaps I did make love to him.

★

The rest isn't important. My husband moved to another city. Let's say, Philadelphia. He went out the front door with a single suitcase and a portfolio full of plans, and that was the last we heard of him. Maybe he found himself. Let's say he met other women: casual mulattas, an elegant Japanese lady, neo-colonialist gringas who soothed their first-world consciences by sleeping with third-world intellectuals, and even Mexican *criollitas* for whom life was a compendium of songs by Joaquín Sabina. Or maybe he just got fed up, locked himself in an apartment in Philadelphia, and allowed himself to slowly die.

★

I bought the *NYRB* at a news-stand and read White's article, sitting on the floor of my empty apartment. White had decided not to reveal the whole story. He had written a long piece explaining that he had made a mistake, that the translations we had previously published with my introductory note were apocryphal, and that, caught up in our enthusiasm, we had fallen into the trap.

During the following months and years, as I learnt much later from snippets of editorial news on the Internet, the mistake White had taken responsibility for, knowing that it would mean the end of his reputation as a publisher (as, of course, it did), provoked an unusual interest in Owen. The translations were published by a large, mass-market publishing house under the name of Zvorsky and, to the extent that books of poetry can be, were a success. The obscure Mexican poet became, in time, the new Bolaño or, rather, a new Neruda. But that day, while I was reading the article in the *NYRB*, neither White nor I knew what would happen about Owen. I tried to call the office once more when I'd finished reading the article but nobody answered. I took a long hot bath.

★

The boy sings to the baby while we bathe her: Autumn leaves are falling down, falling down, falling down. Autumn leaves are falling down and Mama's crying.

★

In that apartment there were no children, no cockroaches, no ghosts. It was on the seventh floor. There was only a bathtub.

★

Pajarote drove me to the airport the next day. We said our good-byes outside. He wrapped a single arm around my shoulders and kissed my forehead. When he'd gotten back in his car, I went into the terminal, alone. I shed a few tears while the lady at the United Airlines check-in counter processed my boarding pass. Just a few. Or maybe lots.

★

I don't know what to do with the three cats who appear to want to move in here permanently. A couple of nights ago I poured whisky into a saucer, thinking maybe that would make them renounce me as the lord and master of their three miserable little lives. But my gesture must have touched them, because the next morning the three woke up on different parts of my mattress and came to lick away my sleep at the stroke of six.

★

I lived a few blocks from Federico García Lorca, but he used to spend the whole day in a student hall at 2960 Broadway, writing his poems. I sometimes bumped into him on the way to the subway and we'd shake hands. He was a plump, pampered little Spaniard, with a tight little ass, who virtuously complained about his Bohemian life in the big city: doves and swarms of coins, buildings under perpetual construction, vomiting multitudes, alienation, solitude. The problem with Federico's poems was that they all ended up being Federiquized. The Spañolet (as Salvador Novo called him) overindulged in his strange metaphors: he converted them into one-way streets, unique systems of equivalence. He liked Harlem and the blacks, he didn't speak English. His parents sent him a hundred dollars each month, which he frittered away in the city bars. I liked the Swedish and Yankee women, I studied English the whole damn day; I liked *tertulias*, café conversations à la Henry James, with generic Aryans – French, German and the speechless, perpendicular, unsociable English, as James describes them.

On one occasion I wrote a letter to Xavier Villaurrutia saying much the same thing, but he never got the joke, perhaps because prophetic jokes aren't funny. The worst defect of the Yankee, I told him, is his incapacity for bad-mouthing people. In a certain sense, I was right. But then, in that life, I was unaware of the

Yankee's most incisive ability – I was living opposite Morningside Park, among blacks who ate watermelon and fried chicken every Sunday (like Mexicans), and an inordinate number of crickets which made the United Estates sound like the main plaza of a town in Sinaloa. The Yankee's greatest virtue – as I now know – is not saying anything; feeding the silence until the other person begins to dig himself a grave in the nearest cemetery, conscious of his inability to keep an appointment at five in the afternoon or to appreciate the joy of Sundays, to be a good sport at all times and so on.

But Federico: the Spañolet and his beautiful asslet, as Salvador Novo used to say.

★

I was thin and lost weight at an incredible speed. I believed in poetry. I wanted to translate my favorite American poets: Pound, Dickinson and William Carlos Williams. I didn't really believe in anthologies, but I wrote to the great Alfonso Reyes, suggesting the idea of a collection of these three North American poets. I was disturbed by the idea that Pound had lived in a cage; that Williams was a gynecologist; and that Dickinson had never left her house. There was a strange correspondence between that constellation of poets, somehow determined by the cage, the house, the vaginas. I suppose that those are the kinds of reasons that matter. But I didn't, of course, mention that in my letter to Reyes, just spoke of the importance of incorporating the voices of those three giants into our canon. When the maestro replied enthusiastically, I dashed off translations of over 200 poems by Dickinson and posted them to an address in Brazil. They probably never even crossed the Hudson River.

I was thin and had long, strong legs, as he probably had. I believed in poetry, but not anthologies. They seemed to me a petty form of exercising editorial power. I just wanted to translate my favorite Spanish-language poets into English. I only once tried to publish my translations. It didn't work out.

★

I printed out the last ten pages to read them aloud, cross out, re-write. By accident, I left them on the kitchen table overnight. This morning I came down for breakfast and found my husband in the kitchen. While lighting the stove to make coffee, he asked:
Why have you banished me from the novel?
What?
You wrote that I'd gone to Philadelphia. Why?
So something happens.
But if I go, there's no sense in writing two novels.
Then you stay.
Or perhaps it's better that I go. Are you letting me go?
Or perhaps you die.
Or perhaps I already died.

★

In Manhattan I died every so often. I believe that the first time it happened I didn't even realize. It was one of those summer days when it's so hot that your brain goes into a bland, boggy state of lethargy which impedes the sprouting and consolidation of even the simplest idea. The brain just burbles. I had to attend to an af-fair the consul considered a top diplomatic priority. A pilot by the name of Emilio Carranza had attempted to fly non-stop from Mexico to New York and the poor man went and crashed into a small mountain in New Jersey. I was asked to write a report on the death of the pilot. It took me more than three hours to pro-duce a paragraph.

When I'd finally finished, I left the consulate in a stupor, feeling terribly sad about the poor stranger who had been splattered that morning. I walked the usual blocks and started down the stairs at the entrance to the subway. That's when it happened. Perhaps I tripped and cracked my head open on the edge of the steps. Afterwards, I must have gotten up, walked to the platform, stepped into the train and fallen asleep in the carriage, because I can't remember anything about the journey. That watchmaker angel who wakes people up exactly at their stations woke me at the 116th Street stop.

The first thing I do remember is the face of Ezra Pound in the crowd waiting on the platform for the train. Of course it wasn't really him. The doors opened and there he was on the platform, leaning against a pillar. We looked each other straight in the eye, as if in recognition, although he couldn't possibly have heard anything about me, a young Irish-Mexican, neither red haired nor good looking, more bastard than poet. I was transfixed – instead of getting off the train, I let the passengers leave and be replaced by others, identically ugly, overheated and ordinary. Pound didn't board the train. He was lost among the crowd of faces on the platform, faces like the wet petals of his poem.

★

Federico had one or two virtues. During my first months in Manhattan we used to see each other every week in a diner over on 108th Street. We met because Emilio Amero, who could never manage to stick one idea to another, had asked us both to collaborate with him on the script of his next film. I don't know what Federico's motivation was, but I accepted because it was a way to speak Spanish with someone from outside the consulate once a week. It was an unfilmable script about voyages to the Moon. I wanted endless journeys in an elevator filling up with eyes; Federico, deeply resentful, rewrote sequences by Buñuel and Dalí in a soft-boiled New York style. And in that way we began to become friends.

We ended up having so little to talk about that Federico decided to invite another poet to join us, in order to criticize him afterwards. To be honest, that's how we began to be close friends. We Hispanics have always been good at that. Spanish is a language which lends itself to fault-finding and for that reason we are bad critics and good enemies of our friends. The poet was a thoroughly decent Yankee called Joshua. But we addressed him by his surname: Zvorsky. And, between ourselves, when he wasn't there, he was simply 'Z'. He had a nose as long and phallic as the island of Manhattan and huge egg-shaped spectacles, which made his face look exactly like the sexual organs of a colt. He was beginning a long poem, as long as Ezra Pound's *Cantos*, he explained. Federico didn't understand a single word of what Z said, since he spoke English as if he were saying mass in Yiddish, so I used to translate for them. Not that I understood much. The poem will be called *That*, explained the poet, because a little boy, when he's learning how to talk and enumerate the World, always says: '*That* dog', '*That* lolly-pop' and so on and so forth. He says his book is going to be called *That*, I explained to Federico, because a little boy always says 'That *perro*', 'That *paleta*' or some such thing.

Federico's second-greatest virtue was that he always got excited when he grasped a new idea. But then straight away he'd be filled with disillusion: that was his greatest virtue. When the Yankee poet had gone, we talked about Gide and Valéry. However differently we spoke the language, as Spanish-speakers, our close ties with Latin and Greek gave us a sense of superiority: we were the heirs to a noble linguistic past. English, in contrast, was the barbaric bastard son of Latin, constantly gloating over its discoveries: the demiurgic function of articles, inventing the world by enunciating it. The only ones worth the effort are Eliot and Joyce, I used to say. And Williams, Pound and Dickinson too. Federico liked Langston Hughes and had just discovered Nella Larsen. Our friend Z was a dog and a lolly-pop but he was also one of the best poets around.

★

Do you think I could have seen Pound in the subway? I asked Federico on the way home after a session at the diner.

How do you mean?

The poet, Ezra Pound.

But he's in Italy or Paris or I don't know where.

He's in Italy, I said, but what does that matter?

Ah, now I understand. Definitely not, it's impossible for someone like you to have seen him.

Someone like me?

★

Homer believed me when I told him I'd seen Ezra Pound in the subway and that there was a woman I kept seeing on another train. What's happening, he said, is that you can remember the future too.

But I had not only seen Ezra Pound. I realized one day, during my comings and goings from the consulate, that for some time I'd been seeing a series of people in the subway, and that they weren't, as you might say, ordinary people, but echoes of people who had perhaps lived in the city above and now only traveled through its overgrown whale's gut. Among these people was a woman with a brown face and dark shadows under her eyes, who I saw repeatedly: sometimes on the platform, waiting, at others on board the train, but always a different one from mine. The woman appeared

89

to me most often in those moments when two trains on parallel tracks are traveling at almost the same speed for a few instants and you can see the other people go past as if you were watching the frames of a celluloid reel.

I wrote a letter to Novo and told him about that woman, who was always wearing a red coat. I told him about her head resting gently against the carriage window, reading, or sometimes just looking into the darkness of the tunnels from the platform, sitting on a wooden chair. I told him about Pound too, and all those people who were and were not in the carriages of the subway, a bit like me. He replied that I was a 'subwanker' and that instead of going around looking for ghosts where there weren't any, I should send him a poem about the subway or something that would fill the pages of the magazine *Contemporáneos*. And I took note and wrote a poem of over 400 lines, because I always took note of what Salvador said. But the brown-skinned woman with sad eyes continued appearing to me up to my last day on the island of subwankers.

★

On the windowsill of the room I used to rent in the building opposite Morningside Park, there was a plant pot that looked like a lamp. The pot had oval-shaped, green flames and there was an orange tree growing in it. Under the meager shadow of that small tree, I used to write love letters to Clementina Otero, the Gorostiza brothers, Salvador and Villaurrutia. I told them about my life in the metropolis, again and again, as if to make it my own, conscious, maybe, that happiness also depends on syntax: Dear X, I live at 63 Morningside Ave, again and again, to each of my invisible correspondents.

★

It's Saturday, my day for seeing the kids. I arrive at my ex-wife's building on Park Avenue and wave to the doorman from the street. He immediately calls up for the children and comes out to smoke in silence with me until they arrive, full of stupid enthusiasm for life. They tell me that their mother has acquired a new radiogram, that she gave them who knows how many new toys, that they watched a war movie in an enormous cinema, and that the following weekend they're going to the coast. I take them, one by each hand, to walk in Central Park.

It's time to go to see the ducks, kids.

We always go to see the ducks, Papa.

So far, I've managed to cover up the problem with my sight. When the sun goes down and things start to hide from me, I say to my little girl: Captain, tell me the English names of everything you can see, and she begins: a duck, a lake, a big tree, a little tree. She pronounces the English words with an exaggerated Yankee accent, as high-class Latin American children typically do. She says: that's a dahk, that's a layk, that's a beeg twee, and that's a lidel twee. And to the older boy, when we're paying for ice creams at the end of the walk, I say: Soldier, count out the coins and give the ice-cream vendor the exact change.

When we're saying goodbye again at the foot of the steps to the building, I give them each a kiss on the forehead with my eyes closed, so they won't give me away – I imagine my eyes like two raisins, grayish, wrinkled, small, rotten. Then I take the train back to Philadelphia. In the carriage, I lean my head against the seat and touch my closed lids to see if my eyes are still there. There they are, brimming with water, with the memory of my children like wounded effigies imprinted on them.

★

It's Sunday and my husband will take the children to the zoo. They'll take a long walk in Chapultepec Park and the boy will come back, still sweaty and overexcited, to tell me about the elephants, who can never go to bed because they wouldn't be able to get up again. Afterwards he'll get a little sad and ask me why: Why can't the animals leave the zoo or you leave the house, Mama?

★

God and people come out in solidarity with victims. Not just any victim, but victims who successfully victimize themselves. My ex-wife, for example. When we got divorced, the *criolla* turned herself into a poet and a victim; the prophetess of divorced poet-victims.

She's just published a small book of deeply embittered prose poems, self-edited and bilingual, with a so-called publishing house owned by her mentor, a French-American poet who runs a writing workshop called SDML (Spiritual Daughters of Mina Loy). I don't think Mina Loy knows about them. My ex-wife has had the discourtesy to invite me to the launch, which is to be celebrated in her own apartment. I know I have to stay in her good books, because if I don't, she'll never let me near the children, so I have the courtesy to go to New York to see her.

A butler opens the door to me. I ask after the children; they're asleep. The apartment smells of a mixture of uptown perfumery, make-up, newly ironed clothes and asparagus. The butler offers me a martini and, of course, a plate of boiled asparagus. My sight might betray me, but I'm still a hound dog when it comes to sniffing out a coven of witches gathered around their bitterness and a plate of expensive appetizers. I hang my jacket up near the door, among handbags and women's coats of every possible size and texture; I accept just the martini and make my way to the salon.

I can't see the women very well, but from the noise and stench they give off there must be over twenty, over thirty of them, sitting in concentric semicircles around my ex-wife and two other speakers – the three witches of *Macbeth*, but more vulgar and angrier with life. Standing facing the room, my balls suddenly shrink. Two peanuts. Perhaps they completely disappear. I stand there behind the last row of seats, as close as possible to the butler, terrified.

My ex-wife is reading in her international Bogotá accent. The poor woman has a very ugly voice – she moans the guttural consonants, elongates the open vowels and squeaks the *i*'s like a badly tuned machine. She reads a poem about the practical utility of husbands. Her mouth always curved slightly downwards when she was reading aloud; also when she was reproaching me for my infinite list of faults. I imagine the bitter grimace, now further emphasized by the furrows and bags of ageing skin. From time to time, bursts of hyena-like laughter break out from the invitees. Maybe, when the ceremony is over, they'll undress me, tie my hands and feet, lift my eyelids and fill my eyes with gobs of spit. They'll shit on me – years of intestinal retention.

She finishes reading the poem and the whole room reverberates with an ecstasy of applause. I reach out my hand to see if the butler is still beside me. There he is. I put my arm round his shoulder:

Don't desert me, brother, stay here close by.

I'll be here, sir, I'm not moving.

She reads another poem, and another. When she's finished the final one, presumptuously dedicated to Mina Loy, the women give her a standing ovation. The chairs scrape against the floor. (Where can she have gotten so many chairs from?) My ex-wife, a spider in the center of her web, looks at me from the opposite corner of the room. I feel her stare. I'm a tiny fly trapped in her sticky universe. The butler removes my arm to attend to the

93

ladies' demands; I stay put, not knowing where to put my free hand; and the one holding the martini is now trembling slightly.

The international Bogotanian starts talking: poetry, the breakdown of identity, life in exile, and who knows how many more *criollo* clichés. She pauses, and to round off says: I'm grateful for the presence of my ex-husband, an unjustly obscure but highly capable poet. The little heads turn in my direction. What does she mean by 'capable'? I get an urgent need to piss. Dozens of painted snouts smile — I can still make out white on black and know they're smiling because the darkened room suddenly lights up like a startoothy sky. The olive throbs in my glass. My organs, in my suit, throb. The faces looking at me throb; out there, the city throbs: the persistent pumping of the blood, the temperature of humiliation. Speech! Speech! I wish for an instant death I am unable to bring about. Then I speak:

I came because I was invited.

(Silence.)

I came because I've always been a dedicated feminist. Viva Mina Loy! Viva!

(Silence.)

In fact, María, I came because I wanted to ask you to lend me just a few dollars to take the children to the fair next weekend.

(Silence.)

★

When I brush the boy's teeth, we count to ten for the middle of the top row, ten for the bottom, fifteen on one side (top and bottom), fifteen on the other. He has tiny, pointy teeth, like a baby shark's.

You've got teeth like a baby shark, I say to the boy.

Do baby sharks have teeth, Mama?

I don't know, I guess so.

But sharks are blind, and I'm not.

I know, I said teeth, not eyes.

Yeah, but still.

Come on, off to bed.

★

I've only ever known a single blind man in my life. He was called Homer Collyer and in 1947, a little after his death and a year before my definitive, fatal return to the United Estates, he gained a fleeting celebrity. But long before that, when I arrived in Harlem in 1928, Homer was living with his brother Langley a few blocks from my apartment, in a mansion on the corner of 128th Street they had inherited from their parents.

Homer was licking an ice cream on the front steps and I went up to ask the way to a church where there was a special service that Sunday that the boys at *Contemporáneos* had asked me to write an article about. Excuse me, sir, where's St John? I asked. He pointed his walking stick towards the sky. I laughed discreetly, but honestly, and stood there like an idiot, waiting to see if, somehow or other, the joke would lead to terrestrial directions.

Did you know that chocolate ice cream is made from cocaine powder?

No, sir, I didn't.

That's what my brother Langley says. Met him?

Your brother? No, sir.

I sat down next to Homer on the step.

He's a good man. A bit of a pig, but diligent in his own way. He says that if I sit in the sun for an hour every morning and eat enough cocaine ice cream, I'll gradually get my sight back.

Well I never, you're blind?

Homer took off the dark glasses he was wearing and smiled at me – he had teeth like a horse's, big, rounded and yellow.

95

I enjoyed long *tertulias* during which I could unfold my ideas slowly, cast scorn on my fellow writers, feel that the world fell short of my standards. Amero used to arrange to meet us in a bar. The owner liked to be called 'Mexico' (he was a very yankee Yankee, who had fought on the side of Pancho Villa in the Mexican Revolution and for that reason alone believed himself to be a metonym for the country). I rarely went to these things, but when I did, I was in for the long haul. The regulars were Emilio Amero, Gabriel García Maroto and Federico, who almost always brought Nella Larsen. Sometimes I joined them, as did our friend Z, who, between whiskies, talked about Objectivism, a word Federico was incapable of pronouncing. He'd say something like 'ohetivicio' and then turn to me seeking complicity.

One night we all drank like ladies and got drunk as skunks. I think Nella Larsen was a bit ashamed of us right from the start, because she changed tables before the floor show began. In one corner of the bar, the famous Duke Ellington, who I had never seen perform before, took the stage. Federico stood up and pulled up his socks. He had short, plump little legs, covered in wiry hair, and the poor guy insisted on wearing Bermuda shorts (a European thing, bloody bunch of fairies). The Spañolet applauded so euphorically that, before sitting down at the piano, the musician tipped his hat and personally thanked him. Federico turned to me as if to say, See? The Duke and I are big buddies. Ellington sat down and began. Z took off his spectacles and left them on the table, among the glasses. García Maroto, possibly the most boring person in the world, listened to the whole thing with his eyes shut, or perhaps he just fell asleep.

During a break in the applause at the end of the first set, Federico put his mouth close to my ear and said: Don't turn round, Ezra Pound's behind you. I rose from my chair so quickly that I almost upset the table. All the glasses fell over, the ashtrays spilled their contents, ice cubes jumped into the air. García Maroto woke up with a start and averted the cataclysm by slamming down his hand, which landed on our friend Z's spectacles, which, in turn, broke. Tiny shards of glass went flying, something like fragments of a child's world: that chair, that man, that poet, that sad, that broken; that sad, broken poet man. Federico cracked up and Z was on all fours looking for the pieces of his spectacles. Fooled you, Mexicanito. What made you think Pound could be here? said Federico between snorts of laughter (his tongue was small, red and rough, like a cat's, and he stuck it out, possibly too far, when he laughed). We made such a scene that a big beefy guy, clearly not overburdened with brains, came up with two other toughs and booted us out. I believe that that night, instead of whisky, they served us hair lotion, because we were all in a frankly hallucinatory state. It's possible that as I was leaving the bar someone stabbed me and stole my shoes and all my money, because the following morning I woke up unshod and without a dime in a hospital in Harlem. That had to be the second time I died.

★

Note (Owen to Araceli Otero): 'I'm not dying so often now. I seem to myself chaste and already modestly strong. I eat very well and am an inconjugatable tense, the future pluperfect. I'm interested in my temperature, but what most interests me about it is what I lose by it, measured in year-pounds. I weigh 124 months. New York is blue, gray, green, gray, white, blue, gray, gray, white, etc. Sometimes it's also gray. (Only at night it's not black.) (But gray.) And you?'

★

My husband reads the children an improving, moralistic book they bought at the zoo about a baby dolphin who loses his family in the sea because he doesn't listen to his mama and papa.

Perhaps a blind shark's going to eat him, speculates the boy. Their voices reach me as if from far off, as if I were beneath the water and they out there, I always inside and they always outside. Or vice versa.

'Baby dolphin starts to cry. He gives a very high-pitched whistle that cuts through the water like an arrow,' continues my husband.

Can arrows cut through water? interrupts the boy. 'The voice of each dolphin is unique,' my husband continues reading, 'like fingerprints.' The boy makes noises like arrows cutting through a body of water.

Pay attention, his father scolds. We're almost finished.

I think about his question.

My husband goes on: 'Mama dolphin hears her baby from very far off. She swims the whole sea in search of him.'

Does she find him? asks the boy.

Yes, look, here on the last page you can see how she finds him.

★

When the children were smaller and we were still living in Calle 70 in Bogotá, we used to play hide-and-seek. I'd hide behind the slender branches of a young jacaranda tree. Where's Papa? I'd ask them. The two would run to me and grab a leg apiece. Here! my little girl shouted. We've found you! said the boy. No, I'm a tree, I'd reply, and lift them up into the air, one on each of my branches.

★

Homer, the blind man, had one eye bigger than the other. One of them, the small one, was permanently turned towards his lachrymal gland, immobile. The larger one rolled in its violet socket like a demented white bird – it was like one of those doves trapped inside a church or railway station, beating its wings against a high, closed window. I enjoyed watching that erratic eye, which didn't see me. Homer would be waiting for me every Sunday with a chocolate ice cream in each hand, at 10 a.m. on the dot. If I arrived two or three minutes late, my ice cream would be half melted, running down his fist.

You're a ghost, Mr Owen, isn't that so? (He pronounced my name the way my ancestors must have done.)

Why do you say that, Mr Collyer?

Well, because I can actually see you.

And couldn't it be that you're getting your sight back from eating so much cocaine ice cream?

No, sir, that's not it. You've got the face of an American Indian but the build of a Jap. And you have the air of a German aristocrat. Today you're wearing a hat, perhaps gray, and a jacket that doesn't suit you one bit.

Don't you like my jacket?

You'd look good in tweed. Next Sunday I'm going to lend you one of my brother Langley's tweed jackets. I'll have to find it and clean it first. My brother's got a lot of things in there.

I never went inside the Collyer residence, although later, when the brothers died and every paper in the city was talking about them, I learned that the house had been slowly filling up with rubbish over the years. Langley had, for some time, been collecting all the papers published in the city and piling them in towers and rows that served as a retaining wall to stop Homer bumping into all the Victorian furniture in the mansion. But Langley, apparently, amassed not only city newspapers but also typewriters, strollers, wheel hubs, bicycles, toys, milk bottles, tables, spoons, lamps. Homer never spoke to me about his brother's zeal for collecting, but now I can imagine that it was not gratuitous. Perhaps he thought that by bringing examples of everyday objects to the house, his blind brother would be able to hold onto a notion of the things that foolishly supported the world: a fork, a radio, a rag doll. Maybe the successive addition of shadows would end by shoring up the thing-in-itself and Homer would be saved from the void which was gradually making its way through his head.

★

Z was a major poet. On one occasion he summoned Federico and me to read us some extracts from *That*. We met on a bench on College Walk, in the center of the Columbia University campus. Federico arrived late, with his habitual star-on-the-verge-of-discovery arrogance. I was with Nella Larsen, he explained, as if to say that he'd been frolicking with the King of France. Federico was like a Narcissus who'd read Freud but, instead of being horrified, had been moved.

Z launched directly into his reading, as do the thoroughly self-confident or those all too unsure of everything. Listening to him read was like witnessing an Abyssinian religious ceremony. I hardly understood anything, even though my English had improved considerably. Some of the poems were riddled with Marxist, Cabetist, Spinozist theories, theories in general, and this allied them to the prophets who used to stand on corners of the Financial District foretelling the end of the capitalist world, of the world as we know it. But beyond the theories there was a plasticity in his poetry that I hadn't heard in any of my Yankee peers (who, moreover, never even suspected I was their peer). Certain lines about how time changes us were etched in my mind. I've never been completely able to understand them, but they return to me from time to time, and they roll me around like a sow in the detritus of her discontent.

Perhaps if I put a bar of soap in their saucer or a bit of shaving lotion, these blessed cats will die and leave me in peace.

★

We play at hide-and-seek in this enormous house. It's a different version of the game. I hide and the others have to find me. Sometimes hours go by. I shut myself up in the closet and write long, long paragraphs about another life, a life which is mine but not mine. Until someone remembers that I'm hiding and they find me and the boy shouts: Found!

★

This Saturday I have to go to Manhattan to see the children. Their mother goes away for weekends – to the luxury beachside houses on the Long Island coast – and I stay in the rich-girl's apartment in the high numbers of Park Avenue.

I arrive a little late and the doorman lets me up to the apartment. I know that there is, though now I have a problem seeing it, a marble table in the hall with a vase of fresh flowers; there's a long table and a room for entertaining guests. There's a canteen of cutlery and the crockery from which I ate many meals, a wall covered in family portraits among which I do not figure – except in the scar made by a nail. There's a piano and its illegible sheet music, trays, a uniformed maid, a bed as vast and bitter yellow as the sea at Mazatlán. There's a cabinet full of all-important spirits.

My ex-wife has had the delicacy not to be there to greet me. She leaves me a note with instructions the maid reads out to me: the boy mustn't eat sugar, for now; the little girl has her bath at eight o'clock. As if I didn't know.

It's a bright, splendid afternoon. I put the note in my pocket, grab a bottle of Colombian hard liquor and take the children for a walk in my old neighborhood.

We want to go to the fair, Papa.

Can't be done, kids, there's no money.

We take the subway to the low hundreds and walk across the city from east to west. On a corner, we buy a watermelon and sodas. When we get to Morningside Park, we sit under an American sycamore, over fifteen meters high, its shadow tangled, like black people's hair. We break the watermelon open with our hands, a stone, a stick and our teeth; I make them eat the whole thing, sitting on our sweaters, because we've forgotten the special rugs their mother keeps for picnics.

We can't eat any more watermelon, Papa, we'll explode, they plead.

Keep eating, nothing comes free.

Nothing except the Colombian liquor, which goes down a treat. There's something miraculous about alcohol for a man in my condition: it unshackles something, relaxes the nerves on the other side of the eyeballs, and allows what for a long time has been hidden behind the cataracts to become visible.

I make out a family a few yards away from us. They've got tablecloths, music, drinks, children with baseball mitts. With my slightly drunk Dutch courage, I approach the group and strike up a friendship with the head of the family. He offers me rum. My hard liquor has all gone, so I accept. I call my children, who hesitate a little before the new clan. One of the younger kids, a sturdy, cheerful girl, introduces herself: I'm Dolores, but you can call me Do. Pleased to meet you. My boy finally agrees to put on the mitt and his sister follows his example. The children play baseball in Morningside: it's a bit like happiness.

I sit down on the edge of a stone from which I can see the window of my old room, in number 63 of the street bordering the park. I can't actually see the window, of course, but it's a scene I know well and can easily reconstruct. Moreover, with every swig of alcohol, a new color reappears, the lost contours of things become sharper. The reconstruction is interrupted, intermittently, by the great breasts of the wife of my new friend. I used to sit at that window writing letters to Clementina Otero; I asked her to marry me again and again. The woman's enormous breasts dance, she dances and eats the last piece of watermelon – our only contribution to the party. My son's made a home run, the head of the family reports to me, and we all applaud from afar. This was where I used to study English obsessively, underlining phrases in the issues of the *New Yorker* the landlady had put in a bookcase together with various editions of the Bible, always the New Testament. The woman bites into the watermelon and looks at me. Hey Mexican poet, she says. Everything slips and slides, and she has a black seed stuck in her cleavage. I can see the seed perfectly and my hook eye fastens on it, something tangible in my planet of shadows. I used to masturbate, I was young, looking at my naked reflection in that very window. The children throw themselves on my son and form a small mountain on top of him: Papa, he shouts from afar, Papa, they're hitting me. She dances, she dances me. The cleavage, the seed, my present-day body leaning towards her, my swollen arms making a grab for her waist, her slaps, You madafaka, my tongue pounces on the seed, follows the soft line of the cleavage, Papa, there was a Spanish poet better than me, he was called Federico, They're hitting me, Papa, the woman tastes of lotion, and there was a very good American poet, his name was Z, a sharp blow on the back of my neck, the paterfamilias hits me again and again with an empty bottle, You madafaka, there's glass everywhere, thousands of tiny shards embedded in my head, everything disappears. The children play baseball and leaves of grass tickle my right ear.

Note (Owen to Araceli Otero): 'The blacks are transparent. At night they dress in glass. I have sometimes walked through Harlem among a river of voices without a course, without a spring (cry that no one uttered). Through them all, the night is visible, transparent… They talk like your Yucatán people. C'mon, c'mon in, misser, two dollahs. One day I went in. It's impossible to write without music and dance.'

★

Who are you hiding from, Mama? From Papa?
   No.
From Without?
From nobody.
If you want to hide, Mama, you have to find a more hidey place.
Isn't the bed hidey?
No, the bed's springy and a bit nuisancey when I want to run.

★

Federico and I decided to found a group inspired by our friend Z. Perhaps at his expense, but not necessarily to his detriment. It was Federico's idea, but I was becoming his sidekick, so I not only agreed, but got fully involved and even contributed some ideas. In spite of his insistence on including Nella Larsen, we finally decided that there would be only two members and that the group would be called the Ohetivices, a word, unlike 'Objectivists', that Federico could pronounce. The idea was that I'd make a quick-fire translation of Z's poems while he was reading them and then Federico would recite or sing them in public places (his theory was that everything rhymes in Andalusian, so it would be easy to keep the spirit and the impossible rhymes of

Z's poems, even, or above all, if we made some purely phonetic translations). We could, moreover, ask for a little money in exchange.

Z, of course, knew nothing of our plans, and thought we wanted just to hear him, so when we asked him to do another reading of the verses from *That* we'd liked so much, he came along to College Walk thoroughly content and well-dressed. This time he explained that in the extract he was trying to make objects speak. I explained to Federico:

He says, here, objects are going to speak.

How can objects speak?

Federico is asking how come do things speak.

Z gave us a slightly paternal look and said, with absolute solemnity: I'm trying to make the table eat grass, although I can't make it eat grass.

What? asked Federico.

He says shut up and sit down on the grass.

Z took out his papers and began to read. The poem began with the rather strange verb 'behoove' and had a rhyme system that seemed at odds with its meaning, whatever that actually was. I think that, more than what his poems *meant*, it was interesting to see what they *did*. I tried my best to translate for Federico: At the beginning he seems to be talking about Hoovers, those machines for vacuuming the floor that make an infernal noise. But he might've said 'behoover', so it's to do with the action of vacuuming, you know how English is always making the bloody nouns into verbs. So the objects ask to be vacuumed by a Hoover, or something like that. And after that there's a bit about whiskying – another damned noun-verb. And then there's some kind of biblical image about infinite locusts. Or maybe it's *locos*. Then it goes: Damn (or perhaps Palm) and something about weed (or wheel). And the line ends: this accordion to fuck-us. (Probably because he'd misunderstood me, that last bit excited

Federico, who was taking careful notes for the next meeting of the Ohetivices). I continued: The last four lines are the ones he read us before. You know, about the way time changes us. They're magnificent. I'd better try to translate them on paper and let you know. In the meanwhile, you get down all the important words and then we'll see what we can do.

The good thing was that as Z didn't understand Spanish, and Federico only pretended to understand me, there was no way I'd end up looking like an idiot.

★

I've decided to name the three little blackguards, who have now taken up permanent residence in my apartment. I don't know if they're male or female and I'm loath to prod their stomachs for fear they'll scratch me if my shaky hand suddenly comes up against a pair of feline testicles. They're called Cantos, Paterson and That. Naturally, I never know which is which, so I sometimes just call out: 'That Paterson Cantos!' and the three of them appear. But those names are too serious to be spoken lightly, so I mostly call them all by their common characteristic: Fucking Yanks.

★

The children play hide-and-seek in this house full of holes. It's a different version of the game. The boy hides the baby and I have to find her.

★

After the incident in Morningside Park, my ex-wife wouldn't let me come back to Manhattan to see the children. You go and get drunk on me, Gilberto, and the children get frightened on me.

The Señora liked that 'me' thing, as if everything were a conspiracy against her person. Some kids went and hit the poor little boy on me and the girl had to find a cab on her own to bring you all back; and you in that state, Gilberto, why do you do these things to me?

The first weekend I should have been with them, they were taken to Coney Island. The children call me from there, with the Sunday pocket money their mother gives them. They know I was born on a Sunday and for that reason alone can get very depressed. That's why they call, they're well-brought-up children: Today we've seen the sideshow with the vomiting dwarf and he reminded us of you, Papa, but smaller. He drank pints and pints of water and then sicked it up into a bucket. It wasn't a trick, Papa, he really did drink and sick up lots. And then Mama bought us some strawberry lolly-pops. But you're allergic to strawberries, Papa, and you could die.

★

I had to tell the boy off for hiding the baby in one of the compartments in the fridge.

★

I've begun to suspect that during that summer of '28 I made a kind of Faustian pact. I can't remember having done it, of course, nor do I really believe in the Devil, Goethe or Marlowe, not even in Thomas Mann, who brought out yet another Faust a few years back. But something must have happened during my successive deaths; something that explains the three-pound fat blind man I am now. It's not that the devil has given me anything in exchange, so I can't understand the scourge of the man boobs nor this so inelegant death.

In that life, hardly anyone had definitively died. Xavier, for example, hadn't, although he would also die every so often. Sitting beside my orange tree, I used to write letters to them all as if we were already ghosts, as if, with my sinking-ship descriptions of Manhattan, I was contributing to the enactment of our future. 'Through the two windows, came the park, full of children's voices', I wrote to Xavier. 'It's a terraced park, like a show seen from the gallery of my window. Here the children are children. The grown-ups kiss, sometimes, when they're not too tired. I'm alone and naked, with only a silk bathrobe covering me': the syntax of aspirational unhappiness.

But one day the orange tree went and died. I'd gone on a trip to Niagara Falls, and didn't water it before leaving. When I returned, it was completely withered – as if years had passed instead of scarcely two weeks. Its sudden, absolute death made me so sad, seemed so prophetic in its way, that I took it upstairs to the roof terrace of my building and abandoned it right there.

★

Mama, guess what I've got in my hand.
  I don't know. What is it, darling?
  An orange tree.
  What?
  Didn't that make you laugh?
  No.
  Well, it didn't make me any oranges.

★

Once, towards the beginning of fall, I was able to see the woman with the dark face and shadows under her eyes for longer than the brief instants our respective parallel train journeys normally allowed us. The doors of the train in which I was traveling had got stuck and we'd been stranded in the station for more than ten minutes. Then another train approached from behind on the adjoining track and stopped next to ours. In the opposite carriage, her head resting against the window, was the woman, wearing an olive-green cloth hat and a red coat, buttoned up to the neck. She was reading a hardback book. By leaning forward a little, I managed to see the title, which, to my surprise, was a Spanish word: *Obras*. The woman felt herself being watched and raised her head – the enormous shadows under her eyes, her enormous eyes. We stared at each other like two animals dazzled by a strong beam of artificial light until her train pulled out.

★

I haven't talked to my husband for over a week. I know he spends the night in the house, because sometimes, when I can't sleep, I sense him getting into the bed. He smells bad. He smells of the street, restaurants. He smells of people. Other times, I know he gets into our son's bed and sleeps there. I hear them getting up together in the morning, taking a shower, having breakfast with the baby, leaving for school. Sometimes, he takes the baby with him for the whole day. At others, he leaves her here with me and doesn't come back until late evening. When he does return, he says goodnight to the children and lies down on our bed to watch television. When I get into bed, he gets up and starts working on something.

This is unbearable, my husband says to me.

I know. I can't withstand it either.

★

Have you ever been married, Homer?

Do you know the difference between analytical and synthetic utterances? he asked in turn.

I'd been silently licking my cocaine ice cream and thinking of telling him about having once wanted to marry a woman called Clementina who didn't love me one little bit.

No, sir, I replied. What is it?

He wiped his hands on a colored handkerchief and began in a professorial tone:

Analytical: utterances which are true by virtue of their meaning. Example: 'Every bachelor is an unmarried man'. Synthetic: utterances which require something from the world to make them true. Example: 'Every married man believes enduring happiness is dancing his whole life with the ugliest woman'.

And which am I?

You're not an utterance, Owen.

★

The boy overheard our conversation last night, and questions me while I get him ready for school.

So who's Withstand, Mama?

What do you mean?

You said something about Withstand to Papa.

Withstand is just a word, my love.

What about 'Without'?

★

Now I am just that: an utterance. And that's exactly why I left my wife, because I wasn't, at forty-something, in the mood for dancing with the ugliest woman. Not even like this, so fat, so blind.

★

Last night I got home, a bit more drunk than usual, from a dinner in the house of the English vice-consul. There was the host, his wife, an Argentinian dandy and three Yanks (men, not cats) with three Yankee women (also not cats, though not far off). The moral problem with Yanks (male and female) is that they think they are Swedes, yet, in certain circumstances, they're just as bad-mannered as Mexicans, but more calculating and hypocritical. We talked the whole night about public works in Philadelphia, the new governor, the dreadful summer climate, the number of flies (male and female), until the dessert arrived and one of the ladies broached the topic of the scandalous infidelity of some famous politician. The gentleman with most seniority, and surely the most experience of the very behavior he was decrying, began speaking. While twisting his wedding ring – as if tightening the screw of an obsolete gear system – he constructed eloquent phrases on the ultimate meaning of marriage vows. Someone mentioned Russell's *Marriage and Morals*. I recalled – I'd read the book in my youth – that the chapter entitled 'Marriage' was followed by another called 'Prostitution'. I said this aloud and everyone looked at me in silence until one of the Yankees, the man on my right, gave a paternal cackle, patted me on the back, Oh, you Mexicans. I felt a desperate need to piss – this always happens when I become the center of attention. One of the wives demanded an explanation, which I did not have to give thanks to the fact that the Argentinian got up to take his leave and eased the tension. The ladies formed a group, the gentlemen lit cigars and, as soon as I could, I also took an effusive farewell of the English vice-consul and his friends, and went out the front door.

The neighbors on his block have rockers and flowers on their porches: probably gardenias, geraniums, petunias. I went up the steps of one of the houses and pissed on some scented geraniums. As I turned to go back down to the street, I walked into a plant pot, which rolled down the steps, spilling its contents. In the darkness, I managed to collect up some of the scattered soil, which I stuffed back as best I could, and, for no other reason than not leaving traces, I took the pot home with me.

I opened the door and greeted the Fucking Yanks. I put my new acquisition on the dining table and pulled up a chair to sit and share the last of the stash of whisky with them. The cats circled, suspicious or curious, I don't know which, around the new object. When I'd set our four glasses on the table and, blindly, poured a tot into each, I put my hand on the plant pot. I felt around its edges, removed the loose earth with my nails. In the center, a shrub was growing, or a small withered tree – a dead orange tree, judging by the trace of a scent, the texture of the trunk and the uneven arrangement of the branches. I touched the container, first with my palms and then with my fingertips. I knew almost immediately that it wasn't just any old plant pot. Running my fingers over the surface, I was able to confirm that it was my pot, the one with green flames, beside which I had penned all the good things I'd written in my younger days. And if it wasn't my old plant pot, it was exactly the same, and that was enough. I was so excited that I kicked the Fucking Yanks around the room. On a piece of paper I found on top of the refrigerator, I began a letter, as if to a dead friend, or perhaps the preliminary notes for a novel.

I read them again today, in daylight with a magnifying glass. The only thing I can make out is: The novel will be narrated in the first person, by ~~a tree~~ a woman with a brown face and dark shadows under her eyes, who has perhaps died. The first line will be these words by Emily Dickinson: 'I heard a fly buzz when I died.'

It was with Homer that I developed my theory of multiple deaths. Or perhaps I should say that it was he who proposed it, and I just elaborated it at his side.

What happens is that people die many times in a single life, my dear Mr Owen.

How come, Mr Collyer?

People die, irresponsibly leave a ghost of themselves hanging around, and then they, the original and the ghost, go on living, each in his own right.

And how can you tell who's whose ghost?

Sometimes it's easy. Physical similarities, especially the ears. Have you heard of a young writer, Samuel Beckett, who published a story this year called 'Assumption'?

No, never.

And the Viennese philosopher who, a few years back, brought out some crazy stuff about language and logic that he'd written in a trench during the war?

Of course, Ludwig Wittgenstein, he's really famous: 'The world is everything that happens'. But I haven't read him either.

Well, it's not important. The other day my brother came home with the newspaper. As he does every day, he read me the society, culture and politics pages. In politics there was a note about Wittgenstein, and in culture one on young Beckett. It seemed to me that both notes were talking about the same person. I asked him if there were pictures of the two of them. My brother confirmed my suspicions: the same ears. We turned the affair over for hours and both agreed: of the two, Ludwig is the ghost and Samuel the original.

But isn't Wittgenstein older?

That's not important.

Huh?

Dammit, Mr Owen. Aren't you the one who can remember the future?

★

The children never come to Philadelphia. Yesterday I sent them a letter saying that Papa was happy and flourishing again, and in the envelope I put a Duchamp-like photo I took of myself, in which I'm hidden behind my plant pot with its armful of dead branches: 'I, a fat New Romantic in a tie, standing in front of my eternal, childless, public-servant-papa writing desk on the coast-less east coast of this genderless country. Papa's missing you both here, Gilberto (2nd January 1951).'

★

The first and last appearance of the Ohetivices was, predictably, a failure. Federico and I found ourselves a nice wide passage in the subway. We brought a low stool on which Federico would stand for the duration of the recital. He would declaim in Spanish while I spoke the lines in English, more quietly, at his side. We also brought a Hoover vacuum cleaner, as we had agreed that this was the object on which the wonderfully obscure fragment of *That* centered. The cue to start would be that Federico pointed to the on button of the Hoover and then:

Federico (in Spanish)	Me (in English)
In this kitchen insane:	This, itching is saying,
'Hoover us,	'behoover us,
Deposit in eaves the things	Dispose us leaves as twins
above happening,	of love opening'
From a wish-turning key	From a whiskying
to fine infinite locusts	to life's infinite *locos*
Damn the jeweled eel, this	Palm or dual wheel, this
accordion to fuckers.	accordion to fuck-us.
No one rarely knows us who	Oh one rarely knows us who
does not touch us,	does not love us,
Time does not do us,	Time does undo us,
we are above	we are a dove
freezing	freeing
Embracing while	Rembrandt's ring
fearing	peering
the guys who choke us	at guises which choke us
So defend eternal men	So deafened, as eternal men
in troikas.'	on vodkas.'

The outcome was the one thing most capable of hurting Federico: no one even stopped to watch us, despite the Spañolet and I having learned our lines off by heart and reciting them with more affectation than an elephant on heat. When I realized that no one was taking any notice of us, I sat on the ground, behind the stool, and started to read – to pretend I was reading – and to savor the letter I would write to Salvador Novo describing the small muscular spasms of the asslet of his adored Andalusian as his whole body and every ounce of charm he possessed strained to attract the attention of the most unmovable race on the planet. Perpendicular people.

Federico had a virtue, or I a defect. Or perhaps it was the other way round. He was not afraid of looking ridiculous. I dreaded it, ended up explaining myself. And there is nothing I abhor more. I get the story all tangled, trip myself up, lose my edge.

That's the reason why I didn't say anything to Federico when I saw the woman in the red coat pass us carrying a wooden chair – slender and a little fragile, like her – but I jumped up, as if someone had stuck a rocket up my ass. I abandoned Federico on the spot and followed her through the station towards the exit. But when she got to the stairs, she didn't go up, didn't go out into the street. She paused for an instant. I waved, but I don't think she saw me, because she turned back into the station.

★

How does this thing about remembering the future work? I asked Homer one day while we were stuffing ourselves with chocolate-and-cocaine ice cream.

You're an idiot, that's what you are. (The expression he used was moron, but as I didn't know the word the first time he spoke it, I wasn't sure if it was a compliment or an insult.)

How come?

You're a novelist, aren't you?

I've written a couple of lyrical novels, sometimes in the light of, at others in the shadow of, André Gide.

Then you're a bad novelist, but you are a novelist.

Given.

If you dedicate your life to writing novels, you're dedicating yourself to folding time.

I think it's more a matter freezing time without stopping the movement of things, a bit like when you're in a train, looking out of the window.

And it's also not unusual that if you're a novelist, you're an idiot.

★

I walked very little in that city where everyone goes for walks. My days went by, bowed over a bureaucrat's desk, composing reports. But one afternoon, while I was eating my sandwich in the kitchenette, I read a news article that put me in such a good humor that I dropped everything and went out to the street. A young husband was asking the Newark district court judge to grant him a divorce because his fiancée hadn't told him until the wedding night that, instead of a right leg, she had a wooden prosthesis. He had stolen the false leg as evidence for his hearing, and she'd filed a suit for robbery. The article stopped there. It was a perfect story that begged an ending, which I would perhaps have written that very night if another story hadn't completely distracted my attention.

I left the consulate in a self-literizing mood and walked through the backstreets of the south of the city, a bit like that Edgar Allan Poe character who chases after crowds without any clear purpose. Turning a corner, I saw a woman. She was one of those Scandinavians who would never join the United Estates upper classes, but who justify all the gobs of oil spat into the sea by transatlantic liners, all the tons of cement poured onto the island of the poor Manhattoes, all the greasy hamburgers, all the toilets, the cockroaches, the truncated vocabulary of newcomers who ask for a sunny-side-up for breakfast. I think that was the third time I died.

It must have happened as I was crossing the avenue towards the corner where she was standing. Most probably one of those demented cab drivers ran me over. Afterwards I continued across and stopped by a streetlamp to get a closer look. She took ten steps in one direction, turned, and took ten steps in the other. Heel toe, heel toe. Always ten. She had bony feet, the color of cream, balancing on dark sandals with two straps that wound round her slim ankles and ended in a bow half way up her calves.

A single one of those legs was worth more than all the others in the city, or in the world. If the poor lame woman who was heading for an early divorce had had at least one of those legs, her young husband wouldn't have felt that he'd been hoodwinked and asked for the divorce. I went up to her and put a hand on her shoulder. She turned, I didn't know what to say – though later I lied to Villaurrutia in a letter: 'She's Swedish and I'm not in love with her, but I had her as a virgin.'

The truth is that Iselin was neither a virgin nor Swedish. She was, to put it delicately, a very hardworking Norwegian woman. But I went down like a rock. I fell in love with her the way a stone might become enamored of a bird. That afternoon she took my hand, led me to a room in a Bowery hotel and had me as a virgin. I stopped being, as they used to say then, a poor cherry, and felt, all 1.45 meters of me, a true macho.

★

My husband doesn't read anything I write any more, it no longer matters to him, it no longer matters. I don't think he cares the least bit about Owen, this Owen, who is perhaps his future ghost in Philadelphia, his future life.

★

My ex-wife wants to take the children to Europe. She thinks that part of the basic education of a good *criollo* is rubbing shoulders with people who are fairer and better dressed. What she doesn't know, what doesn't even occur to the Great Bitch, is that the only thing she's going to achieve with this trip is to sow a little seed of self-loathing in my children. Aware that she would feel some sort of guilt at squandering her family fortune on dresses for cocktail parties that would always end up with her spreading her legs for some dilettante given to murmuring verses by Mallarmé to wealthy Latin American women, I asked her to lend me the Manhattan apartment while she was away. I don't think that's a good idea, Gilberto, she said, with that petulant look of a person who believes it to be her obligation to educate her ex-husband.

★

Note: Owen's grave in Philadelphia has no epitaph. His family wants to transfer his remains to El Rosario.

★

It's the weekends that I find hardest without the children. On workdays I make a coffee at six in the morning, I drink it in the bath, get dressed with the patience and resignation of a father dressing his son, every button a ritual, tying the tie, the pause and a half of knotting the shoelaces. I leave something for the cats, which I imagine the ghosts must eat because a living being would never consume a bar of soap or a pint of cologne. I go to the office, leave, get moderately drunk, alone or with some colleague, and return to the twilight of my apartment full of things the ghosts keep bringing. Today, for example, a bicycle appeared in the kitchen and a tower of books on the windowsill. The same thing every day. Some nights I don't manage to take off my suit and sleep clutching a pillow until it's six again, my alarm clock goes off, and the Fucking Yanks arrive to lick my eyes.

But on Saturdays I don't have the pretext of the tie or the mentholated hope of the shaving cream. I also believe that this is the day when the ghosts go out for walks, because there isn't a sound to be heard and the house feels emptier than usual. I go out too, to buy the papers, which of course I can no longer read properly.

But I hoard them in towers, like the Collyer brothers, and soon I'm going to make a rampart, splitting the apartment in two: I've already got three towers in the kitchen, almost my own height. Before returning home, I buy a coffee on the corner and continue on my way, taking short little slow steps, spinning out as far as possible my return to that world without laughter or quarrels or children crying, longing for at least the ghosts to have come back from their walks. When I arrive, I lie in my Reposet chair and set about stroking the three cats, who jump into my lap as if they were the ones who needed consolation.

★

I returned to the same corner in search of Iselin. She wasn't there. I went back two, three, four times. Her fellow workers weren't keen on giving me a telephone number, an address: Don't get fond of her, kid. At the fifth attempt I found her on her corner. I took her out for dinner in the Bowery. Afterwards, she took me to a hotel. What choice was there?

★

I'm getting attached to the three cats. What's more, they've turned out to have a useful, very supportive side. I no longer put either cologne or soap out for them, just leave my leftovers on the table and they come along to lick the plates. They lick them so well, so thoroughly, that I don't have to wash up anymore. I've taken to stroking them all the time. I like passing my hand from the top of their heads to the tip of their tails.

★

The boy comes into my bedroom, where I'm writing:

Look, Mama, this is our house.

That's pretty.

No, it's not very pretty. A really strong dinosaur came along and the house fell down.

And who's this?

You, you stayed under the roof that fell down.

And this?

It's just a heart that I was painting here.

★

Note (Gilberto Owen to Celestino Gorostiza, 18th September 1928): 'The landscape and all my aspirations are vertical now. These men of the North, mystical, with not the least trace of eye-to-pore sensuality, are just poor musicians. We move around awake, in wide, real space. They in time. New York is a theory of a city built on the foundation of time alone. Manhattan is an hour, or a century, with the woodworm of the subways boring through it, eating it away, second by second.'

★

One day I asked Z if he had ever seen Ezra Pound.

No, he said, but I sent him some poems a few years ago and he published them.

And what would you say if I told you I saw him a few days ago in a subway station?

Well, that he surely will have seen you too.

I suppose the brown-skinned woman used to see me too. Perhaps she even saw me when I didn't manage to see her: when I was absorbed in a book, or fell asleep until my stop on 116th Street. Maybe she also looked for me in the multitude of subwankers and only felt that her idiotic day had been worth the effort after seeing me, even if it was just a flash.

★

Iselin did it like a man. She was a lot taller and stronger than me. When we went into a hotel room she would throw me onto the bed with amazing force, order me to undress, and overrun my naked body with more aplomb than revolutionary troops in a city that has already surrendered – having a naturally small build, I'd learned to be submissive early in life. When she was on top of me, bursting with pre-orgasmic juices, her face had a slight but disturbing resemblance to the Mexican president, Alvaro Obregón, who had died the previous year, so I would grit my teeth and almost always chose to close my eyes at the moment of orgasm.

★

I only leave my bed to make meals for the children, when their father isn't here to do it. I look at my legs, they're like two elephants' trunks.

★

Hey, Mr Collyer?
Yes, Owen.
Do you have a ghost?
Several.
Who are they, where do they live?
With the greatest respect, my dear Owen, what the hell does it matter to you?

★

I considered a speakeasy an appropriate venue for a date with Iselin. As most places of that ilk had permanently closed down in the Bowery, where she almost always suggested we go, I arranged to meet her at the entrance to the subway on 125th Street, near my house. I waited. She arrived late, dressed *à la garçonne*, her hair pulled up under a hat. Manhattan has to be seen from the subway, she said, giving me a tight hug, more fraternal than provocative. The people who see it from above, from the Woolworth Building, don't see anything, they live in a mock-up of a city. Iselin was like a Paul Morand who always got away with that type of pretentious remark just because she didn't really mean it.

We went to a dive on 132nd Street. They sold gin. We didn't stay long because I was sure Nella Larsen would appear and I didn't want to see her. But we drank quickly and well. After the fourth round, my companion gave her hat to a sax player, saying: You're the cat's pajamas, boy. At that time I didn't understand the expression, but something in me did, and my blood boiled with jealousy. I drank too much, hit the sax player with his instrument, took back the hat and died again. I don't know of what, nor did I care: I woke up on the roof terrace of my building, Iselin's boyish hat on my head, her head on my chest, my hand stroking her straight hair strewn across my shoulder. I believe I really loved her.

When she had woken up and we were walking across the roof to go down for breakfast, I noted that the orange tree and its horrible pot, which I had left there months before, had gone.

★

Then I go back to the novel. A vertical novel told horizontally. A story that has to be seen from below, like Manhattan from the subway.

★

Nella Larsen was a writer. She was also Swedish and a mulatta. In that sense, she was a walking, wiggling paradox who united the two characteristics which separated the Owens from the Federicos of this world: the Swede and the African, the world of the whites and the world of the blacks, what was not mine and what was not his. That to which we both aspired in a culture incapable of absorbing us. Nella invited us to a party at her brownstone on the corner of Convent Avenue and 143rd Street. I've only invited blacks, but you, Federico (she pronounced the *d* in Federico as if she were holding a marble between her teeth), are sufficiently black, and you, Gilberto, you look like an Apache or a Suomi, and you have an uglier nose than the average mulatto. Do all Mexicans look that way? Besides, we need a translator for Federico. I smiled at her and said, Thanks, Nella, and then explained to Federico: Nella says that it's going to be all blacks at her party and the only white person will be you.

Federico was mad about Nella's small, perfectly square teeth, her little-boy's pout, the upper lip slightly darker than the lower; as for me, I don't know what I liked. I think, deep down, I didn't like anything. In fact I disliked her. I didn't want to go to the party, but Federico was in newcomer-to-the-city mode and insisted. I don't know why I submitted to the torture of those Harlem *tertulias*: I trotted along to them with Federico like a Chihuahua, and was never more than a remote presence who could neither sing nor dance, only translate and bark a little.

That night at Nella's there was a lot of whisky. We sat around an oak coffee table. Federico was a long way off, on the other side of the room, and I had no one to talk to. I was served a drink that I sipped in silence until, through the arch separating the lounge from the dining room, came a man, thin, very young and very dark, simple in his mannered way. This is a surprise I've brought for you, my darlings, announced Nella, and everyone stopped talking. She turned to me with a half-moon smile: A little Mexican gem, Gilberto, that I've brought just for you.

The guests, uninterested, took up their conversations where they'd left off and the young man came to sit beside me, almost on my lap, and held out a soft hand: José Limón, painter and ballet dancer. Painter or ballet dancer? I asked, and immediately disliked myself. I've never been able to say the things I think in the tone I imagine before uttering them. I think it has to do with not having a good ear. That's why I've always been a bad dancer and never learned to play an instrument. It happens with songs: I hear them perfectly in my head but then I can't sing them. And eloquence of speech comes down to that very thing: being able to say things in the way one imagines them. Limón seemed to be a decent kid. More of a ballet dancer, he said, with a wide, explanatory smile.

José Limón was from Sinaloa, like me, and he'd also left as a young child. He had an affected way of telling his story; he was brimming with self-confidence, as if he knew in advance that his was a trajectory and not just a life; a train that left Sinaloa to arrive somewhere. There are people who are capable of recounting their lives as a sequence of events that lead to a destiny. If you give them a pen, they write you a horribly boring novel in which each line is there for an ultimate reason: everything links up, there are no loose ends. But if you stop them talking and set them to dance or paint, you end up forgiving the ugliness, the foolish expression, the unbridled arrogance of a child prodigy.

Federico began playing a typically Spanish melody on the piano. The guests livened up and took off their jackets. I shrank. Nella sang a little, bending the words of a blues number everyone clearly knew to make them fit into the open-mouthed glass offered by Federico, another super-talented, almost autistic prodigy, now determined to please a bunch of Yankees; blacks, sure, but

Yankees all the same. I shrank even further: a Chihuahua among mastiffs. The Limón kid sprang up, most probably emboldened by the drinks and the general euphoria, and landed by the piano. When Federico finished the last *copla*, he whispered something in his ear. The Spañolet smiled in answer and began to play a waltz.

Limón started dancing, or something like it, and Federico accompanied him on the piano. The guests drew back, forming a semicircle around them; they watched the two of them as you might a family of tropical crabs in a fish tank.

Limón's body moved as if dominated by a horizontal vertigo. His pendulum arms swung with apparent independence around an invisible center of gravity at the level of his navel, legs closely following the gravitational pull of his arms. He anticipated the music only to fall back exactly on the beat. There was a certain sad virtuosity in that thin, compact, brown-skinned body negotiating falls and suspensions with life and death. Federico – it was obvious – was leaving his mouth and soul between Limón's legs.

I was absorbed in the performance, deeply moved, when laughter began to break out among the guests. First timid vibrations of tongues, then teeth and spluttering lips, then explosions from bellies, pectorals, whole bodies languishing in the stridency of a guffaw prolonged beyond that house, beyond that street and that night.

The effects of laughter are devastating, capable of destroying anything which proclaims itself to be sincere, of flipping it over and showing its ridiculous side. I looked away, towards the window, the city and its lights, the darkness surrounding every globe of artificial light. Federico went on playing to the end and Limón continued dancing. When they finished, I applauded enthusiastically and the others started dancing, with Nella again at the piano. Limón disappeared, as do ghosts or the valiant; I stayed in my place on the floor, watching them all dance, clapping obediently at the end of each song, until dawn broke and Federico got me out of there.

So do you really not believe I see my future ghosts in the subway, you Spañolet jerk, I asked Federico on the way home. We were walking south along Broadway, dodging its giant-silver-coin puddles, our weary bodies silhouetted against the almost always sad dawn sky.

I believe you now, Gilberto, Mexicanito, now I do: today we saw my ghost dancing.

A little drunk and with that particularly Latin sentimentality that comes with too much alcohol, I embraced him and said I truly loved him and I hoped that one day we too would be ghosts in the subway, so we could at least wave to each other from one carriage to another for the rest of eternity. God forbid, he replied.

★

Or a horizontal novel, told vertically. A horizontal vertigo.

★

Perhaps the last thing a man loses is his vigor. Later, when that too has gone, a man becomes a depositary for bones and resentment. In another time, I was a person full of vigor, capable of grabbing a Norwegian prostitute by the hand and running along a Harlem street, taking her up to my roof, pulling up her skirt. Iselin also had to be seen from below. Sometimes, I'd ask her to stand on the bed and I would lie beneath her, just looking.

★

I understand that stuff about recalling the future now, Homer.

Congratulations, Owen.

A few months ago I met a prostitute, and the other day we

were on my roof terrace in amorous mode and I was stroking her hair until the sun came up.

Double congratulations, sleeping with a prostitute.

In some way, I knew that in a future I'd remember that instant and I'd know it was the only thing that would justify all my stories of love, and that all the other women would be an attempt to return to that roof, with that woman.

I don't think you've understood the first thing I said.

★

As a form of reciprocity, I suppose, Federico summoned Z and I to the same place to listen to some lines he'd been polishing around that time. I imagined that it would be a simultaneously elaborated and simplified version of another fragment that Z had read about the streets of Manhattan. Up till then, Federico had been writing childish poems about loneliness in the Columbia University neighborhood and his slightly condescending admiration for the blacks. He used to ask me to do quick-fire translations. I would obey, a little ashamed, or perhaps slightly heartened by the idea of pulling down the Spañolet's pants and baring the mechanism of his poetry, which, to my way of thinking, would always be less rich than Z's. But this time Federico read a brutal, beautiful, prophetic poem about a Viennese waltz. There was a museum of wintry frost, a room with a thousand windows, a forest of dust-dry doves. I don't remember much more. 'Photographs and white lilies', ended a line I would've liked to have written myself.

★

A few months before leaving Manhattan, I sent Novo my 'Self-subway-portrait', which I'd spent months cutting and editing, as if Pound and Z and Federico were looking over my shoulder:

Wind nothing more but redirected in
        flute channels
with the sin of naming burning me son in a hanging
        thread of my eyes
good-bye tall flower without fear or stain
        condemned to Geography
and to a coastline with sex your pure
        inhuman vertical
good-bye Manhattan abstraction gnawed by time
        and my irremediable haste to fall
night-darkened ghost of that dreamed river
        found in a single channel
return in the fallen night at the rise and fall of
        the Niagara
let David throw the air stone and hide
        the sling
and there is no forehead at the fore that justifies us
        inhabitants of an echo in dreams
but a sleepwalking watchmaker angel who wakes us
        at the exact station
good-bye sensual dream sensual Theology
        to the south of the dream
there are things ay that it pains us to know
        without the senses.

★

An invitation arrived at the consulate. José Limón and his company are to perform the ballet *The Moor's Pavane*, with music by Purcell. The performance is to take place in the Robin Hood Dell auditorium in Philadelphia. In my capacity as some type of representative of Mexico, it is expected that I go to such events, even though I'm blinder than a locust. I remembered the Limón kid well, how he had so masterfully flopped in a New York apartment, then disappeared for so many years, and who now turned out to be the star of modern dance. And if truth be told, I was very pleased.

We were sent two tickets, so I was accompanied by the consulate's secretary: a plump woman from Oaxaca with a tongue that was never idle. The lights went down and a single spotlight came on, a luminous point in the exact center of the stage. My companion began to narrate the action in my ear (her mouth smelled slightly of rotting lettuce): Now the four dancers are on the stage with their hands linked, two men and two women, the four circling round in a single body. The two men raise one leg really high and then the women. Lovely.

I interrupted her: You don't have to describe every single thing, Chela, just tell me the most important bits and, if you want, I'll imagine the rest.

All right, sir. They've just taken out a really pretty handkerchief and are passing it round between them. I'll tell you when something else happens.

They're raising their legs really high again. Ay, no, sorry, better you imagine that on your own.

It's like they're flirting, first one couple, then another, but it's hard to tell who's whose partner.

After a longer silence, Chela, continued: This is important because you're not going to be able to imagine it: the two men have just fallen to the ground but they didn't make a sound, as if they were light as feathers. Impressive.

The four figures who alternated at front stage were, from what I could infer, characters from *Othello*. The four spectral figures, it seemed to me, were much more like me than the consulate secretaries, than the owner of the supermarket where I did my weekly shop, the guards on the trains, the postmen, the barbers, than my children and their mother in some city in Europe. I suppose, in some way, I'd spent my life dancing round a handkerchief.

The function was a success. As I was leaving the theatre, a reporter took a photo of Limón, the two male dancers and myself. I linked arms with the Limón kid and put on my best smile. The secretary also snuck in, planting herself between the two dancers, and said, Whiskeeey.

★

Romantic endings are never epic. Nobody dies, nobody disappears for good, nothing ever finishes finishing. But I really am dying and people do disappear. The end of my love story with the Norwegian prostitute goes like this: on 29th October 1929 Iselin and I woke up in the Hotel Astor in the Bowery and turned on the radio. Guty Cárdenas was singing 'Peregrino de Amor', which had been released in the summer and was still playing on the radio in New York. I lit a cigarette and said to Iselin: Guty Cárdenas must surely be from Sinaloa. Iselin didn't even know where Mexico was. She wanted to listen to the news. For some days the bulletins had been obsessed with the stock market and its imminent crash. I wanted to cry in peace: for Guty Cárdenas, for whatever. They were going to transfer me to Detroit, and I didn't even know where that was on the map of the United Estates. Iselin remained firm. We turned the knob until we found a reporter. A few blocks from the hotel, according the incorporeal voice, the end was beginning. Enough, Iselin, I said, and tried to retune to the Spanish music station. But Iselin always won: Come on, let's go see what's happening outside, Gilberto.

The streets of the Bowery were empty. We walked a long way, and as we approached the Financial District, we began to hear a desperate buzzing, like hundreds of furious bees. There were people hurrying along, as normal, but now they all seemed like those shadows of people I saw every so often in the guts of the city.

When we were near the stock exchange, Iselin pointed to the sky: a man was leaning out of a window. At that very moment we saw him jump. Or, perhaps, only loose himself, let himself go. The body fell slowly, at first – almost a bird suspended in flight. But before we could avert our eyes, a hat was rolling towards our feet, a shoe stuck in a sewer vent, a leg separated from the rest of its body, the ginger-haired head shattered on the sidewalk. Iselin grabbed my arm and sank her face into my shoulder. Slowly, we continued walking to get as far away as possible from the crowd, which was now forming a circle around the fallen man.

Then I saw Federico. He was sitting on the edge of a bench, euphoric, with a small book in his hand, making notes. We went up.

What can you be writing now, Federico? I asked.

He looked up like an automaton.

I haven't been able to write anything, Mexicanito, only one line: 'Murmurs in the Financial District…'

So what are you doing here?

Well, according to me, I threw myself from the top floor of that building, but it seems I was hallucinating because here I am, talking to you.

I'd like to introduce Iselin.

Who?

Iselin.

What are you talking about, Mexicanito? Are you seeing your subwankers again?

★

There are sweet *tamales* for dinner. The children's father is upstairs watching television while the children keep me company in the kitchen. The baby plays with a saucepan in her highchair. The boy helps me lay the table (three place mats, big plate, small plate, knife, fork, two glasses and a plastic tumbler).

If you want, I can drink from a grown-up glass now, he says, and for the first time I let him.

The baby is hitting the saucepan with a spoon when we start to feel it. Maybe, first, just a sort of presentiment, a very slight dizziness. Next, the internal and then external shuddering of objects. We turn to look, as if to confirm what we are all witnessing. Trembling. Everything trembles, the house creaks, the glasses fall from the shelves and break into so many pieces that the light of the only bulb is multiplied again and again throughout the whole of the kitchen. In some way, that light show is beautiful. The baby laughs. We hear books falling in the living room, first a few and then a cascade. And then nothing. An unfamiliar kind of stillness.

I take the baby from her chair and the three of us get under the table. The electricity cuts out. We stay there, holding each other, under the laid table, silently watching the ring of the stove, where the *tamales* are still heating up.

We see a Madagascar cockroach silhouetted in the flame.

Pa-pa, says the baby.

It's the only thing she can say. Trembling again, this time stronger.

Pa-pa, says the baby, and laughs.

★

Today the children left for Europe with their mother. It was a busy day at the office, so I didn't manage to call them to say goodbye. I issued four passports and signed nine tourist visas. I also received a complimentary photo from the night of the ballet. I quite simply wasn't there. It wasn't that I was out of shot – instead of my body, there was a shadow, an empty space smiling at the camera. I marked my shadow with an X, and went over to Chela's desk to see what her diagnosis was.

Can you see me, Chela?

Of course I can, sir!

No, see me here, in the picture.

No, you're not there, sir!

Was I there when they took this photo?

I can't remember, sir. But don't I look horribly fat next to José Limón!

★

As soon as we're sure the trembling has stopped, we get out from under the kitchen table and head towards the front door. I tug at it, but it's jammed. Nor can we go up to the second floor. I imagine it has been blocked off by the part of the roof that fell in. My husband is there, though we can't hear him, so maybe he's not. Maybe he never was there. We go back to the kitchen, I'm carrying the baby, and the boy is holding my sweater sleeve. There's no running water or gas. But there is a little water left in the saucepan in which we were heating the *tamales*.

★

I left the office a little early to go to a photographic studio. I wanted to have a professional portrait taken so I could send a copy to the children, when their mother calls from some European city with an address. And I just wanted to see whether I'm going mad or blind, or whether I had, in fact, somehow been rubbed out of the other picture. I don't think I'm going blind. In fact, I think I'm going un-blind. But at the same time, I'm disappearing and certain things are being replaced by shadows. Anyway, the owner of the studio sat me on a stool, adjusted it to my height, and asked me to choose between Italian, Swiss and tropical backdrops. I opted for the Italian, though I've no idea what an Italian backdrop should look like. She made a first attempt, and a second. She re-adjusted the height of the stool, tried again. She changed the backdrop. At the fourth attempt, she apologized.

I can't take your portrait, sir, something's wrong with our equipment. You can pay now and come back in a few days.

Why should I pay if you haven't given me my picture?

I think you should pay, sir.

Fine, I'll pay.

★

We also have access to the living room, which connects directly to the kitchen through an arch. The children and I wander like three cats through the jumble of books and other objects, picking up things that have fallen, that fall and go on falling.

★

After the incident at the photographic studio, I stopped off at the supermarket and bought a packet of biscuits, a can of milk for the cats and a bottle of whisky. As I was paying, the thought crossed my mind that, the night he cracked up, Scott Fitzgerald had bought whiskey, with an *e*. I wasn't going to pack a case or go anywhere; I walked home. He had packed a bag and left, driving a convertible, without any set destination. It's easy to imagine that, after hours driving along the pitiless monotony of the highways, he stopped somewhere, anywhere. A motel. With the cash he had on him, he bought a portion of cooked meat, some apples, a packet of biscuits, a bottle of whiskey. I went into my house and double-locked the door behind me. He shut himself up in his hotel room. He knew he'd developed a sad attitude to sadness, a melancholy attitude to melancholy, a tragic attitude to tragedy. So had I.

★

We go into the living room. The floor is covered in books and other things. I put the baby down and let her crawl in the rubble.

★

As I walk into my house, the three cats come to greet me. They take turns to tangle around my legs. I sit at the kitchen table, on which the orange tree stands, dead, then lean across to the fridge, take out two ice cubes, pour myself some whisky and unwrap the biscuits. I open the cat food and the three of them come up to lick the can fastidiously. Fitzgerald knew he had to remember, something that might have been the delayed thud of a punch, the reflected pain of one of those slow but heavy blows that don't come from outside and cannot be foreseen. I eat a biscuit, then another, and don't stop chewing until I've formed a small ball of dough, that is moistened and expands with every gulp of whisky. Fitzgerald had a presentiment. He quickly became aware of his own inevitable disintegration and, all too early, rehearsed his eventual, final collapse. I'm taking too long. I too know that the only remedy is to go on writing. But what the hell am I going to write? I know I want it to be a novel set both in Mexico, in an old house in the capital, and in the New York of my youth. All the characters are dead, but they don't know it. Salvador told me that there's a young writer in Mexico doing something similar. The bastard went and stole my great idea. I put another biscuit in my mouth, the last one in the packet, and call the children from the red telephone next to the fridge, but there's no answer. My

136

palate is burning from the whisky. I should write some notes, here, beside my orange tree.

★

The boy says he wants to play at hide-and-seek in this enormous old house full of holes. It's a different version of the game. His father has to be found.

Shall I tell you what happened, Mama?

What?

The house got bigger, and Papa got smaller, and he has to be found and put in a jar, like a spider or a cockroach.

★

A small, square sheet of paper falls from the withered branches of the orange tree. I take my magnifying glass from my blazer pocket and laboriously read:

Note (Owen to José Rojas Garciadueñas, Philadelphia, 1951): 'It could be my last book. It's going to have a title nobody has used in this century, *The Dance of Death*. I had friends, in the Middle Ages, who showed me how it should be written. They did it pretty well. But I burn much brighter when I write.'

I don't remember having written that. But it's true that I burn when I'm writing.

★

We play. We search for my husband in the living room, among the debris: a Buzz Lightyear, a dummy, a foam rubber brontosaurus, a little bell. We don't find my husband.

137

If I were to write this novel, it would have this line by Emily Dickinson as an epigraph: 'Presentiment is that long shadow on the lawn'.

*

Among the fallen books, we find one of my old Post-its.
    A piece of your book, Mama!
    Let's see.
    Here, you read it out.

Note: As a child, Owen had 'the six magic senses'. He predicted earthquakes. The doctors in El Rosario suggested opening up his head to find the cause.

*

The narrator of the novel should be like an Emily Dickinson. A woman who remains eternally locked up in her house, or in a subway carriage, it makes no difference which, talking with her ghosts and trying to piece together a series of broken thoughts.

*

I don't think Without is in the house any more, Mama.
    Why do you say that?
    Because I think that if he was, he'd help us.

*

One day the narrator of this novel finds a pot with a dead tree on her doorstep and brings it inside. She waters it but it never really revives. She begins to write about what that plant sees from a corner of one of the rooms. The plant will start to impose itself on the voice of the narrator until completely taking it over. The dead tree narrates from a corner, to one side of the front door, from where the kitchen, the small lounge and part of the bedroom can be seen. It likes watching the woman get undressed at night in her bedroom before going to the bathroom to brush her teeth: it watches the tangled trail of her pubis as she passes, then it studies the shape of her ass as she returns to the bedroom.

★

Help us do what?

I don't know, help us find spiders, catch flies and cockroaches, eat cereal.

Would he help us glue the house back together?

Glue the house, Mama, what for?

So it can withstand the next earthquake?

Earthquakes don't exist, Mama.

★

I get up from the kitchen table and head to the bathroom for a piss. I can report, with the greatest certainty a man in my condition is conceded, that I am now positively, absolutely blind. But blindness isn't what I expected. Instead of a definite whiteness or blackness – which would have been a respite from the confusing chiaroscuro of the last months – things are beginning to appear again. Just when I'm starting to disappear. I flick on the bathroom switch. Electric light makes hardly any difference these days and rather serves, as that repugnant German philosopher wrote, to illuminate my almost total ignorance of the world. But on this occasion, the opposite occurs — or, perhaps more disturbingly, the opposite of the opposite. Perhaps this is un-blindness. I switch on the light and see the whole bathroom, the floor carpeted with cat shit, the nearly empty bottles of discarded toiletries, half finished rolls of toilet paper forming a pyramid next to the lavatory, a bottle of whisky in the sink, a creeper growing in through the small window which ventilates the miniscule space occupied by the bathtub. Around me, a score of flies, or perhaps mosquitoes, buzz in the heavy air.

I glance towards the mirror to locate myself within this nightmarish scene. But I'm not there. Instead of my face, I see a flicker of Nella Larsen's. So my theory was correct. This is my blindness. My un-blindness. This is my hell. I turn off the light and unblindly complete my modest hygiene ritual.

★

And where can Without have gone?

I don't know. Perhaps he's on top of the house. Or perhaps he went to Philadelphia with Papa.

Papa's not in Philadelphia, my darling.

Pa-pa, says the baby.

★

Standing by the sink, with the light out, I try to gargle. I can just make myself out in the invisible bathroom mirror. I'm a shadow, with the fading grimace of myself encrusted in the hole where my face used to be. I rinse my mouth and the contact of the cold water with my palate makes me retch. Squatting down, I vomit into the toilet bowl. My face is no longer enclosed by a contour; it extends towards the edge of something that can no longer contain me, like a glass on the point of overflowing. I'm afraid of coming unstuck from myself, I don't want to turn round and spill over, outside my epidermis, like the anti-man in that poem José Gorostiza finally finished, who says he is 'besieged' in his epidermis. What an obscenely clinical word. Why not simply say 'skin'?

The gargling makes me feel sick. I throw up into the sink. If the kids were to see me, they'd say I was the vomiting dwarf.

★

The children and I walk around like three cats in the dark corners, picking up things that have fallen and go on falling. The baby crawls happily on the floor carpeted with books.

★

One of the cats, most probably Cantos, my favorite, is waiting for me outside the bathroom door. I feel quite moved. It's as if it understood that something was happening to me. That things aren't going very well today. I try to stroke him, and as I slide my damp hand gently down his spine I realize that he no longer has a tail. Has he been fighting with That and Paterson? Bastards.

★

Mama, says the boy, looking out of the living-room window into the patio, come and see.

What is it, my boy?

A little cat without a tail!

There is indeed a tailless cat walking around the patio as if it were the most natural thing in the world. It's a disturbing sight. I take the two children back into the kitchen. We're safer there.

★

As I cross the living room to return to the kitchen, carrying Cantos in my arms, I see Ezra Pound, clear as daylight, sitting in my Reposet, making notes on a piece of paper. Above his head, flies are gyrating in perfect circles, tracing a vortex. He's focused on his task, and I don't want to disturb him for fear of interrupting some important, or at least clever, poem. I pass him in silence, and enter the kitchen once more.

★

We're not going to leave the kitchen any more, I say to the boy. It's too dangerous. If there's another tremor, things could fall on us.
  Houses, Mama?
  Yes, houses.

★

Back in the kitchen, I pour myself a little more whisky and search for That and Paterson under the table. There they are, the catty things. I feel for their tails: nothing. How can three cats suddenly lose their tails? Not even a stump, a scar. Nothing. Just round little asses and thick fur where formerly there were tails.
  I begin to write the children a letter that I'll send when their mother tells me where they are: If they tell you I've died, kids, it's a lie, I'm just fading away. The doctors say I'm going blind. But that's not true either: what's happening is that I'm rubbing myself out. And it's not just me. The cats of this world are also rubbing

142

themselves out. Watch out for their tails during your trip. You'll see that some of them haven't got any. Did you know that was possible? I didn't. But even if I'm rubbing myself out, you two will always be able to see me if you want to. Anyway, what's true is that I'm potbellied. And that I live with three tailless cats you'd really like. Their names are That, Paterson and Cantos.

★

There are cockroaches in the kitchen. I don't know what's happened, but they're everywhere. Maybe our neighbor's frogs died in the earthquake and the cockroaches have multiplied. Maybe they've always been there, under the house, and have now come up through the rubble. The boy and I squash them under the soles of our shoes.

★

If I could talk to Homer once more, I'd start:
   Can I ask you a question, Homer?
   Fire away, Owen.
   What's the last thing to disappear?
   I'm not sure what you're referring to, Owen.
   To death, of course.
   Did you know that certain animals can exist without their heads?

★

While we're treading on insects in the kitchen, the boy tells me that if you cut a cockroach's head off, it goes on living for two weeks. He says he learned that at school. I get a fit of giggles. So does he. The baby doesn't laugh: she gazes at us in serene silence.

I believe I would have preferred just to go blind. Unblindness and disappearing, erasing myself while I begin to see others clearly again, doesn't seem to be the best way to end my days. I'd already gotten completely used to the idea of not seeing anything or anyone. And now what happens is that Nella appears to me in the bathroom. Pound in the Reposet. A while ago, I thought I heard, very clearly, the slightly nasal voice of Guty Cárdenas singing '*Un rayito de sol*'.

From my briefcase, I take out the picture of the evening of the *Moor*. I'm sure I was there, I remember it. In any case, I don't think I'll go back to the photography studio. I don't want to leave the house. In fact, I think I'll call in sick tomorrow.

★

We've finally finished killing all the cockroaches. I tell the boy to get under the table. We're going to make a bed and sleep here, I say.

★

Someone knocks. I get up from my chair and head to the door of the apartment. As I begin to open it, I hear a din like thousands of cockroaches' tiny feet going up and down the stairs of the building. A slow, paralyzing fear settles in my stomach and seeps down into my limbs. My legs become rigid and a tremor shakes my hands. I double-lock the door and head to the bedroom, sliding one hand along the wall of newspaper that now almost completely covers the left side of the passage.

★

Why do we have to sleep under the table, Mama? Can't we sleep on top?

No, it's dangerous. We're going to sleep under it.

Like cats?

Yes, like three little cats.

★

I go into the bedroom and Federico is shaving his legs by the lamp next to my bed. Beside him, sitting at my dressing table, Z is cleaning his spectacles. I don't say anything – I was brought up to believe it's always better not to make waves, although my first instinct is to tell Federico it was about time he got rid of all that leg hair. They're taking up all my space. I hurry back to the kitchen, pour myself a glass of water with an inch of whisky and gulp it down. The cats are under the table. Maybe I can lie down on top of the table, next to the orange tree. That way I can think about the novel a little longer. Maybe I can try to get some sleep.

★

I try to get some sleep under the kitchen table with the two children huddled against my body, covering each of them with an arm. I'm afraid of the darkness because the cockroaches might come out for a walk and we won't see them. I'm woken by the sound of their little feet, scratching on the cement or the metal of the fridge. I cover the children's ears so the cockroaches can't get in, so they can't get into their dreams.

What's that noise, Mama?

Nothing.

★

I take off my blazer, fold it to make a pillow and get onto the table.

★

I think it's the cockroaches, Mama.
  Or maybe it's your papa.

★

As I lie in the darkness of the kitchen, eyes wide open, I hear the buzzing of a fly. Or maybe a mosquito. The sound turns into the distant siren of an ambulance that never quite arrives, returns to being a fly, and goes back to being a siren. I can't see the mosquito or fly, of course. But when it comes close I swat it. I wonder if this is going to be my last handle on the world: a Doppler effect that comes to nothing, that never finishes. I sweat, tremble, turn over on one side on the hard wooden surface. William Carlos Williams comes in through the door and says:
  I've spent the whole day delivering children in ambulances. Why don't women give birth in hospitals any more?
  I don't know.
  If you don't mind, Gilberto, I'll just use your sink to wash my hands.
  Go ahead, William. Or is it Carlos?
  I take my blazer from under my head, cover my face with it and try to sleep.

★

No, Mama, it's flies. And mosquitoes. During the day, they hide inside the shower and at night they bite us.

It's terribly hot in the kitchen. I uncover my face. William Carlos has finished washing his obstetrician's hands and is watching me, standing at the foot of the table, like a surgeon about to begin his rounds. I say:

What do you think of this couplet I just wrote? Dead fly song of not seeing anything, not hearing anything, that nothing is.

Not bad. A bit like Emily Dickinson, but not bad.

He checks my pulse and tells me I'll be OK. Then he leaves the kitchen. I cover my face again. The flies or mosquitoes are still buzzing nearby.

★

The baby has woken up and is crying. The boy and I try to calm her.

Cradle her, suggests the boy.

Cradle her?

Yes, to see if it calms her down.

I rock her in my arms. Nothing. She keeps on crying. Her sobs fill the room. We get out from under the table and walk around the kitchen.

Why don't we sing to her, Mama?

★

I think the mosquitoes are voices. I can distinguish two: one belonging to a little boy, and the other to a baby. The baby cries a lot and the child sings a disturbing nursery rhyme.

★

The boy sings. He has a beautiful, tuneful voice: Autumn leaves are falling down, falling down, falling down. Autumn leaves are falling down and Papa's missing.

★

I don't want to hear anything, song of not seeing anything. Beside me, in the white darkness, I hear a soft laugh, the merry chortle of a baby. I feel the blazer that covers my eyes rising, the heat of the room entering and shaking my body, the excited voice of a little boy beating my face:

Found!

ABOUT THE TRANSLATOR

Christina MacSweeney has an MA in Literary Translation from the University of East Anglia and specializes in Latin American fiction. Her translations have previously appeared in the short story section of www.booktrust.org.uk and in *Litro* magazine. This is her first translation of a novel.